EVOLUTION

a novel

EVOLUTION

a novel

Ken Barris

Published by Zebra Press
(a division of the New Holland Struik Publishing Group (Pty) Ltd.)
PO Box 3103, Halfway House, 1685, South Africa
Tel: (011) 315-3633
Fax: (011) 315-3810
Email: zebrastaff@icelogic.co.za

First edition, first impression 1998

ISBN 1 86872 248 1

Editor: Dineke Volschenk
Designer: Micha McKerr
Cover design: Micha McKerr
Cover photograph: Hein von Horsten/ABPL

Reproduction by Positive Proof c.c.
Printed and bound by Creda Communications, Eliot Avenue, Epping II, 7460

To Roy Davies

Acknowledgments

Eugene Kruger's discussions on evolution are drawn largely from *Evolution: The History of an Idea* by Peter J. Bowler (University of California Press, 1984) and from Jonathan Howard's lucid and economical *Darwin* (Oxford University Press, 1982). While I have tried to represent their arguments accurately, it must be borne in mind that particular ideas have been taken out of context and subordinated to novelistic ends. Koen Sieberhagen's anti-Semitic cartoon was originally published in a Greyshirt publication, *My Ontwaking* by JHH de Waal, Jnr, and reproduced in *Between Crown and Swastika: The impact of the radical right on the Afrikaner nationalist movement in the fascist era* by Patrick J. Furlong (Witwatersrand University Press, 1991, p.59). The inscription on a Yorkshire church plaque quoted by Deon Viljoen is taken from Alan Paton's *Hofmeyr* (Oxford University Press, 1964, p. 320). The enquiry into Eugene Kruger's teaching of evolution echoes the indictment and certain of the argument in the trial of John T. Scopes, particularly the arguments of Clarence Darrow and William Jennings Bryan, as related by Scopes himself in *Center of the Storm* (Holt, Rinehart and Winston, 1967). I have made analogous use of the mission statement of the Potchefstroom University of Higher Christian Education, though there is no intention whatsoever to reflect conditions at that university.

Finally I thank Professor Richard Mendelsohn of the University of Cape Town, and Dr Clive Glaser, formerly of the UCT Oral History Project, for information on aspects of historical method. I have tried to present that information as an undergraduate student such as Jessica Kruger might see it; however, I am clearly responsible for any naivete shown in this regard.

That it shall be unlawful for any teacher in any of the Universities, Normals and all other public schools of the State which are supported in whole or in part by the public school funds of the State, to teach any theory that denies the story of the Divine Creation of man as taught in the Bible, and to teach instead that man has descended from a lower order of animals.

That any teacher found guilty of the violation of this Act shall be guilty of a misdemeanor and upon conviction, shall be fined not less than One Hundred ($100.00) Dollars nor more than Five Hundred ($500.00) Dollars for each offence.

The Butler Act of 1925, quoted in *Center of the Storm* by John T. Scopes (Holt, Rinehart and Winston, 1967)

Die Potchefstroom Universiteit vir Christelike Hoër Opvoeding streef in sy opvoedkundige taak na die wetenskaplike toerusting en algemene vorming van die student tot vakkundigheid, roepingsvervulling en diensbaarheid waarin skoling vanuit die Christelike perspektief en waardes sentraal staan.

From the current Mission Statement of the Potchefstroom University of Higher Christian Education.

Jessica

Cape Town/Franschhoek/Pniel, 1996

1

A smell of dust dominated lecture room 1-01. Light from the fanlights fell on my pad. Amateurish sketches of giblets, kidneys and lungs tumbled down the page, leaving little room for sentences. On the worn podium below, Teboso Ngqayimbana held his clouded spectacles at arm's length, peered at them and spoke: 'In the past, the gentle art of haruspication was often resorted to — by Etruscans, you know, primitive Europeans. They would cut open a goat and read the future in the steaming, odorous and bloody mess of its intestines. More accurately, they would divine the true condition of the present. Now we consult our own — entrails, that is. Little has changed except that we have dispensed with the goat. We don't need goats, no. Instead, we talk to our own guts.

'My friends, you needn't look so puzzled, I said "gut" — we talk to our gut, not our goat. And what do we say to this gut? We ask it questions, you know: How do I "feel"? Am I "okay"? What "wound am I wounded with" this morning? "Who am I" this particular Tuesday? Yes, write it all down, provided you keep that suspicious look on your faces.'

He laughed, a series of esses.

I carried on doodling. My face, I could feel, was so suspicious it set my teeth on edge. This man was beginning to affect me. What was it? I probed at it like a sore tooth. His love of words — his own — irritated me. He basked in them, he rolled around in them, they made him glow.

But I enjoyed his thinking, I admit that: one of the few lecturers who didn't bore me.

After the lecture, he asked, 'Is there a Ms Kruger here? Ms J. Kruger?'

I raised my hand, but he didn't see it. So I went down the aisle against the stream of students making their way out.

'Here. I'm Kruger.'

'Ah, you are Ms Kruger.'

Again, a flash of irritation as he repeated what I had just said. I waited, arms folded over my cloth bag.

'I wanted to see you because I'm marking your most recent assignment, and I was very impressed by your work. It's certainly well beyond what I'd expect of first year standard.'

'Thank you. I'm not first year.'

'Well, that explains it. What are you then?'

'Third. I'm doing this with my majors because I needed to get some idea of anthropological methods.'

'Ah yes, I see. Well, congratulations on your essay. It was a pleasure to read.'

I coloured. 'Thank you,' I said tersely, and walked off.

I was supposed to have coffee with my friend Natasha Goldman. She was late, of course. I picked up a cup anyway and sat down and stared across the cafeteria. It smelt of doughnuts and stale oil. China clashed loudly. A single fly buzzed around my cup. I kept brushing it away. It came to rest on a spill of sugar, rubbing its forelegs together, gloating.

Natasha stood in front of me, breathless, still wearing her sunglasses. 'Sorry I'm late,' she said, seating herself.

'How do you know it's me?' I asked.

She looked at me blankly. I reached across the table and lifted the Ray-Bans, setting them back above her hairline. 'It's dark in here. You don't need them.'

Her eyes were troubled. She turned away. 'I do,' she said. She snapped the glasses back, then she took a piece of sugar-free gum out of her bag. Her hands trembled slightly as she unwrapped it, and stuck the slab halfway in. She left it there, the rest sticking out like a spare tongue.

'I'll get you some coffee?'

'Please,' she mumbled, the gum wagging up and down. Then she sucked it all in.

I got the coffee, and more for myself, and returned. As I walked back my heart started thudding loudly. I thought I knew what was coming; it had been building up for some time; I didn't want it to come.

Sliding under the tables onto the benches without breaking your knees is an art, especially with two cups of coffee and a pile of change in your hands. I managed it, then said hastily, trying to fend it off: 'Why does he irritate me so much? Why, Natasha?'

'Who?'

'Ngqayimbana.'

The Ray-Bans looking at me made me feel more uncomfortable. I felt scrutinised. Then I started blushing again, and stared down at the table, fixedly: at two cups of coffee and four hands, young women's hands, hers bearing many rings (even on her thumbs), mine bare.

'He irritates you because he's an intelligent black man and you're an unreconstructed racist bigot and you can't bear it.'

'Nonsense, Goldman! You're talking nonsense.'

'Alright, I'm talking nonsense. Then I say he's an intelligent man and you're an unreconstructed feminist bigot and can't bear it anyway.'

I knew there were droplets of moisture on my forehead and dabbed at them with a paper napkin.

'That damn music,' I said. 'How can they play Frank Sinatra in here?'

Green lenses stared at me pitilessly. It was still coming then and my heart must have been shaking my chest and shoulders visibly. For a while I couldn't breathe. At last I reached forward and took off her damn glasses and placed them firmly on the table. They rested against her hands, tanned dark above, and what I could see of the underside was coral pink.

'Natasha, stop being —' it burst out '— the sexual Gestapo.'

Her face, taken by surprise: suddenly wounded, dark eyes framed by dark rings and a wide sympathetic mouth turned down in unrestrained, unfulfilled passion.

'Sexual Gestapo,' she said, hurt. She placed her hand across her breast, fingers spread out. 'And you know I'm Jewish and you say such things to me, Gestapo.'

But I knew she wasn't joking, and she knew that I knew, and we both knew that sooner or later she would tell me that she loved me and wanted to express it fully. Not now though. She was too hurt. And I? Sipped chicory and looked at her through distant calculating eyes, cruelty being a shield for my easily penetrated skin.

Later, when I had time to feel, I wondered if I could, if I would enjoy it. I realised guiltily that maybe the answer was yes on both counts; but it would make life so complicated, for all her passion and dark beauty.

Ngqayimbana. His name slid off my tongue like a lizard's tail discharged, writhing in furious panic. I sat on a mattress at a party at Arno and Geraldine's house in Rondebosch East, my back to the wall, and said: 'Ngqayimbana.' Softly, curiously, to myself. I said it because he was also at the party and because I was drunk on several paper cups of Roma White. Though we hadn't made any contact, I watched him. His forehead glistened. He was short and wore round owl glasses. His shirt buttons were popping open downwards, threatening to reveal his drumlike paunch. As it was, I could see tight black curls on his chest. He was a marathon talker, and his hand rose and fell in the smoke like a plied spade, tireless. I hated what I saw and enjoyed hating it. Somewhere along the line enjoyment crowded out hatred but both were there (where? in the spaces between my teeth, in the soft palate, in the lower crease of where my breasts sag, in the web between the outer toes of my left foot, in the roots of my ever self-betraying scalp, etc). When the mattress dipped beside me under his weight I wasn't surprised; I was just drunk enough to be psychic.

'What does the J stand for?' he asked.

'J? What J?'

'Your J.'

I was still staring down into the nearly empty cup. 'Jessica,' I said eventually.

'Jessi-ka.'

'Don't click my name like that!' I heard my name gurgle, amused contralto. A wave of sheer hatred broke over me. Self-hatred, probably. I glowed bright crimson. I was sure he would feel the heat radiating off my face. I still stared into the bottom of the cup (round and white) but I could sense his colour. It was golden, the kind of lurid gold you find in a Beacon chocolate wrapper.

'I click your name because, because it is a stronger name that way, and it goes with the way I think you are.'

A smell of cane spirits rolled across to me, not disagreeable, but strong, concentrated. I looked at him at last. No, he wasn't golden, just an ordinary chocolate colour like his voice. It gave me the courage to believe I wasn't bright crimson after all.

'And what way,' I asked carefully, 'do you think I am?'

'I have some vague notion, but I need to see your palm. To make sure.'

'I don't believe this.'

'No, seriously. I read palms, it's state of the art in the human sciences.'

I think he took my hand more than I gave it to him.

'Really? State of the art?'

He nodded.

'Jessica Kruger,' he said leaning back against the wall, my hand still captive.

'You're not reading my palm,' I objected. My hand was beginning to panic and from it waves of repulsion and anger began to travel to more inner centres of my body: 'Your eyes are closed!'

'Braille,' he said.

'Braille?' This time my voice shrieked high; I quaked; I took my hand back and wiped my eyes. He laughed gently — yes, a series of whispering esses — and I said, 'You're a chancer, you know that.'

'I only form hypotheses, all the time hypotheses. They must be tested against the flux of what really occurs.'

The music blared incredibly loud, then someone turned it down again. Some joker playing Bing Crosby. It sounded like 'che wawa che wawa che wawa mai bambino cuchala gimbo'.

'Seriously,' I resumed, 'if I am to be an hypothesis, what is the content of this, of this — hypothesis?'

'Jessica Kruger, refined to hypothetical expression, by all means. Let me see. Palm?'

'No.' Fuck off, I thought and shifted further away.

'I would say,' he continued, elucidating, elucidating, 'I would say that Jessica Kruger has a kinaesthetic response to the world. She feels colours. She tastes shapes. She thinks with her body.'

'How do you know that?' I heard my voice bleat, querulous: 'You've got no right to say that! To know that, I mean.'

'From the way you write. It's not really appropriate to academic writing, but you make it work surprisingly well. I enjoyed that quality in your essay rather than the academic content.'

'Thanks so much.'

'Hypothesis two.' My eyes snapped open. His flickered over my face, as if painting or digitising it perhaps. 'Jessica Kruger feels crowded a lot of the time. She feels terribly crowded, yes.'

'By what?'

'By the images her body transmits to her head, by the people around her who spark off those images.'

I was beginning to smart and said: 'Now what makes you think that?'

'I see it in your — in your —' he crowed with laughter — 'body language.'

I felt myself drawing in like a slug or snail touching salt. My lips threatened to tremble — oh, not with tears but with discomfort and tension. I wasn't enjoying this anymore.

'Hypothesis three — is it four? Jessica Kruger —'

'Stop it.'

He raised his hand, palm towards me: 'Only guessing, only guessing. I'm a student of phrenology you know, I read the bumps in your face and skull. I like a legible face.'

That hand came towards me and traced a curving line down my brow, temple, cheekbone.

My reaction was complex. I hate it when a person sees into me. I fear it. I don't like being touched sometimes. Then there was the surge that the sight of him filled me with, a kind of bleeding at the gums. I didn't understand it at all and I was actually shaking as I said in a low voice, 'Go away, Mr Ngqayimbana.'

He responded with a dignified nod and said, 'I must respect your wishes,' and left me alone.

Che wawa che wawa che wawa mai bambino go to sleep, said the music. Che wawa che wawa che wawa mai, bambino close your eyes. It wasn't Bing Crosby, it was Perry Como singing a secret language that only men understand and use to control everyone who isn't a man.

2

I sat on Jameson Steps waiting for Natasha. Not even ten, the sun was beginning to beat down. It was a clear day, and I could see the Hottentots-Holland mountains in wonderful detail. I had nothing to do until she arrived. I read the mountains. We've been here a long time, they said. We're a much greater work of art than anything by Michaelangelo. You think we're tons of stone, but under the skin we're dragons, serpent bones clawing our way out of earth, monstrous figures thrashing about in a slow frame of time. You only imagine we're mute and still ...

She arrived in Paco Rabanne glasses and sat down next to me, took out one of her Vogue Slims and put it in her mouth. She lit it and sucked in, exhaled hot sunlit smoke.

'Sorry,' she said.

'Sorry? Sorry what?'

'Sorry I'm late.'

'You're always late.'

'Smoke?' she asked, offering me one of her cigarettes.

'No thanks. You know I don't. Why are you offering me smokes and apologising suddenly for being late? You don't normally.'

Her hand touched down on my leg, just above the knee, and rested there. I didn't want her to do that, but I left it. She said, 'What a mood you're in, darling.' It was her right hand. The cigarette stuck up between her ring and middle fingers, not much thicker than the lead of a clutch pencil. I took it out and lifted it to my own lips, sucked tentatively. I didn't inhale, just tasted. I tasted a trace of her scent on the butt.

'I think,' I said, 'this stuff goes in through the skin of your mouth. I'm sure I felt a rush. A little tiny rush even though I didn't breathe it in.'

'Well, don't try inhaling then, you'll go *rushing* down the steps screaming hysterically.'

'That's exactly what I feel like doing.' I inhaled theatrically. It hit me like a slug of tequila. 'Dangerous,' I said, 'dangerous.'

Her hand came off my knee and she took the cigarette back. She smiled and said, 'Irresponsible child.'

'I have this ridiculous history project,' I said, changing the subject. 'We have to do a family history. Can you imagine anything more boring? I have to go and research some real family history. Weird. I don't ever think about my family. I mean my forebears, my ancestors. Now I have to go and research some of them.'

'Horrors,' said Natasha.

'Mind you, we do have a family skeleton in the cupboard. I think there's a scandal of some kind in the past. A love affair or something.'

'Oh, that's more promising. Who loved whom, and what was so scandalous exactly?'

'I think it was my grandfather and the maid. I'm not sure. I'll have to ask my mother.'

A shadow fell across us. We looked up at a portly figure standing between us and the sun.

'Jessica Kruger,' said Teboso Ngqayimbana. His voice was surprisingly meek. 'I wanted to speak to you. Outside the environment of the classroom, that is.'

'Speak to me.'

He gestured vaguely: 'I would like to speak to you in more private circumstances. Could we perhaps go and have some coffee?'

'I have a date right now. With my friend here.'

'Oh, I'm sorry, I don't wish to intrude —'

'That's no problem,' interrupted Natasha. 'We were going to have coffee just now anyway. Why don't you join us?' She smiled unctuously at me and turned again to Ngqayimbana. 'Really, why don't you?'

He shrugged and chuckled, as if his good intentions not to intrude were utterly defeated. 'Well,' he said, 'if you're sure you don't mind?'

'Not at all,' she said glibly, sticking out her hand. 'I'm Natasha Goldman.'

'Delighted,' he said, holding it limply and releasing it. 'Ngqayimbana,' he added. 'Teboso.'

I could swear the woman gushed: 'Oh, the famous Mr Ngqayimbana. I've heard so much about you from Jessica!'

'Is that so?' he said, smiling brilliantly. 'About me?'

I stared at her in surprise: it was completely untrue.

'You're not one of my students?' he asked Natasha, suddenly anxious.

'No.'

'Ah, I am relieved. Then I am under no tremendous compunction to have recognised you — which I didn't, I regret to say.'

Compunction? What did he mean? Compulsion?

'It's the story of my life,' Natasha replied darkly. 'My own mother has trouble recognising me.'

'Quite,' he replied absently. Then he turned to me: 'The reason why I wanted to speak to you privately — or at least semiprivately as it were — is because I wished to apologise for last weekend. When I reviewed my behaviour I felt most uncomfortable with myself. I believe I exceeded the bounds of discretion, you see.'

'So you did,' I said dryly.

'What did he do?' asked Natasha. 'This sounds too interesting.'

'He did my astrological chart,' I replied. 'He read my palm. Psychic readings, you know; unsolicited, but psychic.'

She took it literally: 'Oh, you do readings?'

'No, no,' he exclaimed with a fat chuckle. 'I had the bad taste to explain to Ms Kruger how I believed her to be constituted. I was quite incorrect from beginning to end. I believe I upset her a little.'

I felt myself glowing crimson again.

'Ah, you were Macbeth,' said Natasha, her voice turned as camp and admiring as it could go: 'And you unseam'd her from *nave* to *chops*.'

'Something like that,' he said modestly; and my discomfiture turned into bloody rage. I sat still, paralysed by the flood of it. I'm not sure how the rest of the conversation went. Perhaps I even took part. Looking back, it was the smug, self-congratulatory nature of his apology that inflamed me.

'Then I am forgiven?' he asked me.

'Of course,' I replied blandly. 'Nothing to forgive at all.'

'Well then, I don't wish to intrude further on your conversation with, ah, with your friend here.'

'Natasha,' she said. 'My name is Natasha.'

'We must talk some more,' he said.

'Sure,' I replied. Something tugged at me, a dim sense that he genuinely wanted to make contact.

He left. I waved and said, more to myself, 'Tugboats in the night.'

'What's that?'

'Nothing, Natasha. Nothing.'

'What a charming man,' she said.

I realised that I was still staring at her face. Her cheek-bones to be more exact. I realised that they reminded me of slices of cling peach.

'Did you say something?' she asked.

'No, nothing,' I replied. I realised that some things were best left unsaid.

How did I get myself into this? Red silk hangings, the sonic attack of a Chinese soprano and her steel banjo, odour of abalone, ginger and fried leeks, Coke in the traditional phallic bottle. But that's not the question. The question is: how did I get into this with Teboso Ngqayimbana?

It was his voice coming over the phone at four on a Saturday afternoon: 'I wonder, Ms Kruger, if you would mind dining with me tonight?' It had a sibilant penetrating quality, and I had been woken up from an afternoon sleep and was sluggish and dull, and couldn't find the wit to say no.

Now I sat facing him in the Silver Dragon Restaurant in Observatory, watching him expostulate, watching the tasseled lamp in miniature glint from the lenses of his spectacles, watching the sheen on his forehead, watching his hand wave thickly: 'You should try their twenty-year old hedgehog nest soup, Ms Kruger, I have eaten it once and I can vouch that it is delicious, delicious.'

I felt vulnerable and brittle waiting for the waves of repulsion to break out, but they hadn't so far. My nerves held an uneasy truce with Ngqayimbana.

I asked: 'Is the soup twenty years old, or is the hedgehog's nest twenty years old? Or the hedgehog itself?'

'I'm not sure, Ms Kruger. I think it is a peculiarity of the sign system that you say it like that.' He laughed, esses uncoiling.

'Your voice sounds like a cash register,' I said. 'An old-fashioned one.'

He laughed again, gaily, and said, 'Try some of the shark fin wun tun. Here,' spooning crisped ears of batter curled about pockets of unspeakable meat into my bowl. 'I believe shark is banned as a food in Japan because of the high mercury content. In the sharks' livers, that is. They eat anything, no matter how polluted.'

I paused, my mouth open.

'Not to worry,' he said, 'this restaurant uses only good cold Atlantic sharks. Puritan sharks, I'm sure, predators from beginning to end, eating only tuna and dolphin. Not scavengers. They spit out the divers they catch, unless they're Africans.'

'I want to ask you something, if you don't mind.'

'Please, ask by all means.'

'Why do you keep calling me Ms Kruger?'

'The last time I called you by your first name, you took offence as I recall.'

In my mouth: buttery crunching of wun tun, flash of rancid meat. 'Oh no, that's not true,' I cried. 'I took offence at a whole lot of other things. It wasn't my name.'

'Well that may be, but there are other reasons. I want to keep a suitable distance between academic faculty and student, to avoid any suggestion of the improper.'

I'm sure my mouth dropped open. Did he mean it? Belatedly I saw the glint of amusement.

Now the waiter bought new dishes, piping hot, and a bottle of red wine Teboso had ordered.

'Oh, Ms Kruger,' said Teboso, 'you must try some of the pork foo yong. This abalone sauce goes with it nicely.'

I did, I stuffed it in, trailing streamers of sweet cabbage, my breath sucked away by pungent mollusc vapour.

'Teboso,' I said (when did I start calling him Teboso? How did it happen?), 'there is something I wonder if I should tell you.'

'What is that?' he asked dreamily. Chopsticks rose to his mouth, dangling a fragment of glossy roasted pig. He sucked it in.

'It's a bit personal.'

'Go on, tell, tell.'

'I can't.'

'Why not?'

'Oh, this is too embarrassing.' And of course my dreadful betraying blood rose to my face.

'Please don't be embarrassed,' he said, grave now. 'I assure you that there is nothing about you I could ever find embarrassing.'

He leaned back and gazed at me, calm and benign. He took off his glasses. I think it was the first time that I had ever seen his eyes without them. I thought he looked kind.

'You have a strange affect on me,' I said at last.

One of his eyebrows went up very slightly. I couldn't speak about it anymore. He waited. 'And?' he asked finally.

'Nothing,' I said. 'And nothing.'

The waiter was back again with more dishes, steam escaping the salvers. We retreated into food. Such copious, excessive, ribald food. I sucked at a knucklebone. It came back to me then: 'This effect,' I said. 'This effect.' I blurted it out: 'You make my head spin. I really don't know what to say. You disturb my relationship to reality.'

I wanted to say: It's like a fever. But I didn't. Fever has too many of the wrong connotations.

All he said was, 'Uh-huh, uh-huh,' rapidly. I didn't know what to do with that answer. It sounded like he agreed with me and in fact expected it.

I boiled with sudden resentment. He tucked into his bowl seriously for a while and ignored me, and spooned in another helping.

I snapped: 'And for God's sake stop calling me Ms Kruger.'

As I said it, a fine crack suddenly appeared in my wine-glass, running vertically. Wine seeped out, dribbled down the stem, spread in a widening shadow about the base.

I watched it in surprise; my hands seemed disconnected from my mind. Teboso gazed as abstractedly at the slowly falling level in the glass and said, 'You know Jessica, there is something truly intimate in the use of a first name. I hesitate to use a first name unless we have come to the place in time to use that name. It's like kissing someone. We kiss strangers, you know, we kiss anyone these days. It's your mouth you know, that's very personal.'

He reached forward and sprinkled not nearly enough salt over the dark stain.

And then he said: 'You have an effect on me too, Jessica. I think I want to be your friend. If you don't object too much.'

I shook my head.

With that settled, he said: 'Just now we shall have sour glazed plums and golden butterflies.'

I think he meant bowties.

I dreamt about him. I dreamt he sat cross-legged opposite me with a translucent bowl of tea steaming between the spatulate fingers of one hand, a joint in the other. He sipped and puffed alternately. The seeds had been left in the joint — I could hear them pop as it smouldered — and his eyes were extremely bloodshot. Why the joint? I suppose it symbolises his confounding vertiginous impact. He confronts me, drugged and bloodshot, a Bacchic beast. But the tea forms a still, convex space leaving so much in it unexpressed. At some point the joint and tea vanished from the dream, leaving behind mixed textures, harsh and fine. These twisted together in our conversation, in our interaction, which became intimate. That's all I want to say. I have conveyed the gist of the dream, but I write the next sentence with difficulty. Only my hypocritical honesty forces me to set this down: I woke up coming.

3

Natasha and I sat under a grimy cypress tree on what my mother tells me was called Freedom Square in her day, a small patch of grass from which the rest of the University of Cape Town spreads out. 'Will you come with me?' I asked. 'I don't feel like facing him alone. He's supposed to be quite fierce.'

'I don't mind,' she said. 'Let's have lunch in Franschhoek first to build up courage. Then we can interview the fierce uncle Koen.'

'Great-uncle. He was my grandmother's brother. He must be very old now.'

She lay back on the grass and wriggled her hips. 'I just can't get comfortable. What sort of fierce?'

'I'm not sure. I think before the war he was a Greyshirt.'

'Greyshirt? What war? The Boer War, I suppose?'

'No, Natasha. He's not that old. He'd have to be about a hundred and twenty. I'm talking about the Second World War.'

'Oh, that war.' She sat up again, brushing dry grass off her hair. 'Greyshirt?'

'It was a right-wing organisation in the thirties. They were Nazi sympathisers. Something like the Ku-Klux-Klan, only they didn't have pointy heads. At least Koen hasn't. His head is quite normal.'

'What are you dragging me into, woman? Do I need to visit a Nazi sympathiser? What if he puts me in a concentration camp?'

'I'm sure he wouldn't put a friend of mine into a concentration camp.'

'I'm not convinced,' she said. 'But I'll come if you buy

the lunch. It might be the last meal I'll ever have.'

'Don't be so neurotic, Goldman. I bet he doesn't even have a concentration camp.'

'Well,' she said grudgingly, 'maybe.'

The letter I had been waiting for arrived at last:

My darling Jessica

It was wonderful to hear from you again. I hope you won't think I'm complaining if I say that I wish you would write more often! I know we speak on the phone quite regularly, but there is something quite irreplaceable about a letter, about the art of writing letters in general I mean!

Your father asked me to respond to your query about our 'skeleton in the closet'. We don't really know much about it. Your grandfather Eugene was a taciturn, pessimistic person; his last years were quite depressed, and I can't say that I got to know him at all well. As far as we know, he never kept a journal or diary, so there aren't any documents in the possession of the family that could help you. We don't have any letters that bear on the subject either.

I don't think I have to tell you that there is hardly any point at all in trying to ask your grandmother. I suspect that Anfra retreats deliberately into senility when it suits her, rather like the famous case of elderly people who are selectively deaf. Please don't repeat this remark to your father! He feels she should be treated with more compassion than I can summon for her; I don't think he realises just how manipulative that woman is. I did try to ask her about it, but she refused to understand what I was talking about. Well, she didn't exactly refuse. She just went passive and pretended I wasn't there. I accept that these memories might still be painful, but I wanted to throttle her nonetheless.

In any event, this is what we do know: back in the thirties, Eugene and Anfra employed a domestic worker by the name of Jolene Galant. Your grandfather grew rather attached to her! (Please forgive my euphemisms!) It appears that he was helping her with some or other correspondence course, and he and Anfra were going through one of their periodic 'difficult times' — I always think it's a pity people were so reluctant to divorce in those days, don't you? — and one thing led to another.

By the way, I know her name because I actually found a photograph of her in a trunk of your grandfather's possessions, and her name is on the back. I hope you appreciate the trouble I took for your history project! I spent a morning in the garage, which I rather enjoyed, getting enormously dusty and sweaty. You have no idea how hot it gets in there. In any event, I pass it on to you as we have no need for it.

As might be expected, the secret leaked out and there was a most horrific scandal. After all, this was not only a love affair, it was love across the colour bar! (I suspect that things would have been much better if it were merely a sexual episode). I believe that the marriage was shaken to the core. It obviously survived, though as we know Anfra and Eugene did not have a good relationship thereafter. (Perhaps they never had a good one in the first place, I don't know.) When you come back for the holiday you can quiz your father about this matter. As you know, he still complains most tremendously about his parents' bad relationship and all its diverse ill effects on his precious constitution, even though he's over sixty.

Soon after the events in question, Jolene Galant disappeared. I don't know anything about the circumstances. You could ask your uncle Koen if you can bear to speak with him, as he was alive at the time, and perhaps he had something to do with it.

I hope this information is helpful, paltry as it is. We are longing to see you again, and please write every so often!

With fondest love

My mother, quite typically, had forgotten to enclose the photograph. It arrived a couple of days later with a scribbled note of apology. Here in this small, slightly blurred monochrome rectangle was my first image of Jolene Galant: standing before the camera, smiling tensely, holding a coffee pot on a tray. Her discomfort, the poor photographic quality, the scratches, failed to obscure her beauty.

Perhaps beauty was too strong a word, but I was drawn to her. The picture hinted at high blank cheekbones, dark eyes, full lips — an elusive sensuality transmitted over the six decades that separated us. The structure of her face suggested San or Khoi blood. She must have been about my age when she fell in love with my grandfather, if that is in fact what happened.

I turned it over. As my mother had said, her name was there, very faded, the handwriting cramped and illegible. Beneath it were a couple of lines that I couldn't read with any certainty. The second last line was a single word that I guessed was 'Pniel'. An address? She had probably lived in the hamlet near Franschhoek. Finally, the year, which was 1937, the one fully legible term.

At first the picture gave me a sense of security: here was something solid on which to base my research, the first icon through which the past might express itself concretely. But the more I studied it, the more daunted I felt.

The road from Paarl to Franschhoek was startlingly beautiful. It was a long time since I had been there; I had last visited Koen when I was about thirteen, and remembered very little of it. We crossed the Berg River on a railway bridge; the old road bridge had been washed away, and no one had ever fixed it. The road simply detoured up to the railway line, and we drove along the sleepers, the car drumming on the beams.

'This is like *Deliverance*,' said Natasha. 'Soon we'll find a little retarded man playing the banjo better than Pinhas Zuckermann. What will we do then? We'll have to shoot him with an arrow!'

'What are you talking about, Goldman?'

'I'll have to keep my sunglasses on.'

'What? What are you talking about?'

'He mustn't see that I'm Jewish.'

'Who, Koen?'

She nodded.

'Well don't say anything then.'

'Bitch.'

I drove on.

'Look, there's Pniel!' she exclaimed.

'What's Pniel?'

She twisted round in her seat and looked back. 'It's a town. I saw a sign that said Pniel.'

'Oh, that Pniel. I think it's a so-called coloured township that used to be a missionary station.'

'What do you mean "so-called" coloured? Is your uncle "so-called" Afrikaans? Is your boyfriend Teboso a "so-called" Zulu?'

'He's not my boyfriend,' I said doggedly, trying not to blush. But the heat rose off the back of my neck. Natasha tilted her head and inspected me critically.

'Flushed again, are we? The truth always comes out, you know.'

I ignored her till we reached Franschhoek.

French and German tourists everywhere, busloads of them. Buses crawling up the two miles of restaurant-crowded road, belching diesel, belching tourists. Tourists walking up and down in the blinding light, dragged down by cameras, chattering unintelligibly, bemused and broiled. Natasha and I became tourists. We strolled about the Huguenot Monument, shuffling along behind the others, admiring the long rose gardens, the dressed granite arches, the flat, not quite vernacular buildings — no, not admiring, not seeing. This was a territory and we were in it, tourists of an ideological monument that preserved and projected Afrikaner Nationalist history in a certain light. But the world surrounding it had changed, leaving this island of granite forms and yellow roses isolated in time, a curiosity.

We stood below the statue of a Huguenot woman looming over her lotus pond like a ship's figurehead; only it was a granite figurehead.

'It's not really a monument to the original Huguenot

settlers, is it?' Natasha remarked. 'It's more about the Afrikaners who put it up in the forties.'

'She's quite good-looking,' I said. 'I think if I saw that woman in the street I would think she was lovely.'

'Proud and handsome,' said Natasha, 'horribly confident.'

'Horribly? Horribly confident?'

'A woman that beautiful and confident makes decisions. Her decisions stick. She makes decisions about other people.'

'What decisions?' I asked, stupidly.

'She decides who's going to go into the concentration camp.'

'Oh, Natasha,' I said, looking up at the proud granite cheekbones, the sensual granite lips.

'Aryan,' said Natasha. 'A mother of the *herrenvolk*.'

'That's a bit harsh, don't you think?'

She squinted up unhappily at the statue and said nothing.

We had lunch in a delightful garden, in the shade of old and expansive plane trees. She refused to come with me to Koen, so I left her there and went to visit him on my own.

A lull in the conversation. Time slowed down, gracefully allowing me to observe his head as if it were a sculpture, a bronze set free of motion and change (yes, his head seemed to glow copper; I suddenly imagined it to be a kind of prototype on which all Afrikaans heads and faces were modeled). Something shark-like about the jaw, the wide mouth, though all his features were dried out, shrunken by his great age, the skin worn fine and turned to parchment rather than leather. His eyes reminded me of a shark's too — dulled, knowing very little. But then attention returned and when he looked at me, I felt the blunt force of personality.

'I'm surprised you came to see me, Jessica,' he said, in Afrikaans. 'Your side of the family hasn't contacted me for a terribly long time. I'm afraid it's for political reasons.' He laughed, that self-deprecating touch of the very old, knowing they're regarded as insignificant.

'I think we visited you about ten years ago, Oom Koen.' Normally I addressed my older relatives by their unadorned first names; in this room of antimacassars and chiming quarter-hours, it seemed rude to do so.

'Yes, yes. You did. I recall I had an argument with your father that day. He said the Nationalists would surrender power within my lifetime.' The old man laughed again. 'I said to him: "My lifetime? You must be mad! Maybe young Jessica's lifetime, but never mine!" And now look what that fool De Klerk has done. Your father was right, but please don't tell him I've admitted it.'

He smiled at me. It seemed that the river of his political animosities no longer ran so deep.

I took a recorder and pad from my bag. 'Oom Koen, can I tell you why I came to see you?'

'I thought there must be a reason. Go on.'

'I'm doing a research project at university. It's an oral history project. Basically, the idea is to get information not from documents, but from interviews. You know, with people who were actually alive at the time, survivors of the period who remember —'

'You've come just in time. I won't be a survivor very much longer.'

I smiled. 'So if you don't mind —'

'You know, I don't remember much. About anything. I don't remember much at all. But of course I'll help you if I can.'

I sensed that he didn't often get visitors, and that long hours passed in his sitting room without diversion. But I had left Natasha at the tea garden nursing a bottle of champagne, and didn't want to stay too long. I pressed on: 'Thank you. The thing I'm researching is —'

Suddenly I wasn't sure what I was researching. The history of my grandparents? Their personal lives, their careers? The private fact of a love triangle? As I talked, trying to explain myself to myself as much as to Koen, he seemed to grow more and more troubled. Perhaps he was annoyed by something I had said. I was puzzled by his reaction. My uncertainty grew until I stopped and said: 'Am I making sense? I must really be confusing you.'

'No,' he replied gravely, 'I think I know what you mean — Jessica, please — will you do me a favour? Could you make us a pot of coffee? It's the maid's afternoon off and I find it difficult.'

'Of course, Oom Koen.' I went to the kitchen, wondering what offensive thing I had said or done.

When I returned with the coffee, Koen had fallen asleep. I stood in the lounge, tray in hand, staring at him indignantly. Was he really asleep? There was something about his breathing that made me suspicious. But why on earth would he close the interview in such grotesque style? He did look fragile, his head lolling to the side, his mouth slack. I didn't want to wake him, if indeed he was asleep. I left a note thanking him and promising to return.

I was disorientated by my uncle's odd behaviour. I stood outside his house, in the shade of an avocado tree, listening to the trilling of the cicada, suffering the invasive heat, the alien energy of the place. I felt mildly faint, then had a sudden and bizarre feeling that I was not myself, that a stranger stood in my place. She could have been standing in a garden in another country, a place with a history barely connected to my own life. She/I bent down to the garden tap and drank sweet water. Slowly, slowly, my sense of normality returned as both countries slid together and merged: the country of the past, the one I called my own. I recall that I almost staggered as I took the first steps to the gate. Vertigo.

4

I picked up the phone, dialled, and slammed it down the minute it started ringing. I wouldn't do it. I was not interested. I paced around, then opened the door and went out onto my balcony. I stared over the roofs of Observatory. Why shouldn't I? Why on earth shouldn't I? I went back in and dialled again. I forced myself not to put the phone down though I felt sick with anxiety. Pubescent cow, I thought.

He picked it up and said: 'Ngqayimbana.'

I hate people who answer the phone abruptly.

'Is that Teboso Ngqayimbana?' I asked, mealy-mouthed.

'Ngqayimbana,' he said again, rapidly, affirmative in tone. 'Who is that?'

'It's me. Jessica.'

'Oh, yes.'

'I'd like to come and see you.'

'Oh, yes.'

Oh, yes? Was that all? Time stretched itself out maliciously, joining me to Ngqayimbana by a telephone line but nothing else. We breathed at each other. I wanted to slam the phone down, to break even this tenuous connection.

'Hullo?' he said.

I gathered my courage: 'It's about a project? If you could help me with certain aspects?'

'Sure,' he said, 'nine tonight.' He rang off before I could respond.

I put the handset down, smarting with resentment and feeling that I had made a terrible mistake. I had entered a strange middle ground, seeking him out for advice on an academic matter not connected to his subject, visiting him at his flat rather than his office: it was all so sneakily obvious.

Nine precisely. Here comes the time-conscious European student with ulterior motives (a journey to the interior). She stands at the door and rings, two melodious Joshua Doore chimes. The door opens. What beasts unknown, what barren landscapes, what precious minerals to be vouchsafed? Here comes Teboso Ngqayimbana to make open his realm.

'Oh, yes,' he says, bluntly. He adds: 'Jessica Kruger.'

I sat carefully on a brown Joshua Doore couch. The man had no taste at all. There were three china ducks on the wall in descending order of size to suggest the vanishing point, each one an obscene chartreuse. My back was very straight. I watched him intently, his movements triggering waves of adrenalin and subcortical alarm.

'Tea?' he asked. 'Coffee?'

I nodded. He continued to peer at me through smudged glasses, his eyebrows raised. I cleared my throat and said: 'The latter.' He still peered at me, I remained motionless. Two flies caught in amber. His left hand was held in the air, slightly higher than the right. His ears were like that too, one slightly higher than the other. 'Coffee,' I said. 'Please. Coffee.' He nodded and swiveled, his hands thickly parting the air, rowing him towards the kitchen.

I leaned back carefully against the plush sofa and was swallowed whole.

I interrogate myself: is it true that black men have giant penises? Will I emerge bruised and clubbed? In my mind's eye, assegaais and zebra-hide shields flash, and ostrich plume headdresses and monkeytail aprons swirl. Somewhere in the back of my mind, Michael Caine in a red jacket grimaces heroically, but too late to save me.

My ears itched frantically. I sat with my hands in my lap, demure, silent, suffering. A train approached on the nearby southern suburbs line, filling the flat with its dingy rhythms. The sound receded.

Teboso returned with a tray of what proved to be expresso. Its smell filled the room, royal and demanding. I sat deep in the seat, my back pressed against the foam: delicate cabbage butterfly, wings spread wide and pinned to a cork board.

My cup rattled on the saucer. I reached forward and steadied it with my free hand. 'What is it, Jessica?' he asked. 'What can I help you with?'

I explained. I didn't really listen to his answer which took the form of a monologue, one which didn't apologise for its length. I watched the movement of his hands instead. I wanted them to touch me. He sensed my tension because he interrupted himself to ask, 'Am I making sense? Does this answer your question?' And I said, 'I hang on your lips, Teboso.' I said it with such intensity that he was startled and lost his train of thought. His gaze turned inwards as he recovered it, then turned back to me. My eyes moistened. I saw him swallow. Would his voice never dry up? It made my head spin. Then he tailed off, spread his hands wide like a lay preacher and said, 'Come, Jessica Kruger.'

I stood up, my frame quaking with the force of my heartbeat. He directed me to the bedroom, his hand in the small of my back causing me to sink ever faster, spine broken.

There was a ghastly huge mirror on the bedroom wall, almost as big as the window. I saw our dual reflection and looked away quickly.

Nothing could stop the seminar. He sat on the side of the bed and said, 'Jessica, I think you're focusing on the wrong thing here. Sure, I know, you're doing a project on your family history. But look at the larger context.' He took his socks off. 'Where do you place your family in the broader social and political history of the time? What were the values of the community in which they were enmeshed?' Then came his trousers. His briefs were the same red as Archbishop Tutu's robe. 'You could explore the assumptions of privilege your forefathers no doubt sported, their awareness of caste and racial status.'

'It's tactful of you not to mention my own assumptions

of privilege,' I said gingerly, resting my back against the cold wall, my hands crossed on my lap, eyes averted from the mirror.

He laughed, hissing like an unusually cynical lizard, and continued: 'I think you should make this a history of the maid.' He began unbuttoning his striped shirt.

I reached out and rubbed it: 'Feels like Woolworths.'

'Woolworths? No, I think it's Cape Union Mart. Yes, that's where I got it.'

I stretched my feet and curled my toes, so creating waves of violent sexual feeling, that traveled up from my feet. I stopped at once and let out a shuddering breath. 'The maid?' I asked.

He said with sudden energy: 'The maid is the kitchen window, you know, into the oppressor's home.'

His shirt was off now. He had heavy shoulders, big male breasts hidden in curly fur, his belly was larger than I had anticipated.

'That's what I would like to read into your work,' he said. 'Otherwise you make a trite account of events concerning only your family. Go to the local township there. Don't make official history, there is enough of that.'

And then he was naked, apart from his spectacles.

'Oh, God,' I said and leaned forward suddenly, greedily. Tugboat Willie, I thought, helplessly taking in so much, so much.

I was in the bath when the bell rang. 'Who is it?' I shouted. I thought I heard Natasha's voice. Cursing, dripping, draped in a towel, I went to let her in. It was after midnight.

Yes, it was Natasha, bearing a bottle of Cordon Negro Brut; a friend stood behind her, partly concealed. She said, a trifle apologetically, 'It's too late, isn't it?'

'Not at all!' I exclaimed, assuming gaiety to cover the despair I really felt, my own voice raking over the ashes of my feelings. I stood aside to let them in; we crowded the minute passage; I found it hard to breathe; then we moved through. I excused myself and hid in the bathroom. As I stared at my bleak face, at the rings under my eyes, I heard the champagne cork pop. 'Jesus,' I muttered, got dressed again, smoothed myself over and went out.

'I'm sorry,' I said to the friend, 'didn't catch your name?'

'This is Jean Camoens,' Natasha answered for her. Jean said nothing. She was a vaguely attractive thirty-five year old in denims and neat white platform shoes. She had a careful face, precise mouth, sprinkling of grey in conservatively dressed hair.

'Jessica,' I said. Jean smiled. I sat down.

The black champagne bottle stood on the table between us, isolated, erect. 'I'll get glasses,' said Natasha brightly. Jean and I sat waiting, her face not quite serene, not quite smoothed over into a smile. She leaned forward slightly, her hands resting on her thighs. I coughed into my palm.

Natasha returned with three glasses and filled them. She thrust one into my hand, and said, 'To us.'

I lifted my glass mechanically and said, 'To us.'

'No darling,' said Natasha, 'you should say "To you," not "To us." I mean to *Jean and myself.*'

She sat back and rested her hand on Jean's thigh. Their fingers twined together and Natasha looked at me, chin slightly raised, not quite silently gloating.

'To you,' I said, unable to deal with my mixture of relief and jealousy.

Jean almost smiled.

Natasha took a long, appreciative sip and sighed. 'You look like shit, Jessica.' Then she stared critically at her glass and said, 'The mark of a good champagne —' her cheek bulged over the impress of her tongue — 'The mark of a really good champagne is that it tastes like aspirin.'

'It's true that I'm not at my best,' I admitted.

'And what is the problem? Tell aunty natasha everything.' Her voice had taken on a hard edge as she camped it up, creating a kind of weapon.

'Nothing I feel like talking about right now,' I replied. I

looked down into the mouth of my glass, taking refuge there.

But Natasha wouldn't be put off. 'Let me guess now, let me see if I can put my finger on the matter. It wouldn't have anything to do with your friend Teboso whatsisname, would it?'

I kept quiet. Then, as a diversion: 'Jean, what do you do?'

'I'm an accountant.'

'Oh, that's interesting.'

'No, not really.'

Natasha plunged into the ensuing silence: 'Jessica, I do think you're avoiding my question. What are we to make of this?'

I think my eyes pleaded with her, and I despised myself for it. But it was like the smell of blood to a predator. Her expression sharpened — a psychic pricking of the ears — she seemed to listen to things inaudible, waiting for her moment.

'How did you meet Natasha?' I asked Jean.

She waved her free hand vaguely and said, 'Oh, we've known each other for a long time.' Then with a very modest smile: 'She takes me out of the cupboard for a while every so often.'

'My dear, how can you say that?' exclaimed Natasha. 'We are an *item*!'

I caught her watching me — to see the effects of her statement, I suppose. We both looked away, quickly, furtively.

Natasha resumed her interrogation. She said, 'Your problem, Jessica. We were talking about your problem. Yes, it's got to be the Teboso. Ah! There goes the famous blush! Jean, do you see that blush? Do you see it? My dear, what did you let him *do* to you?'

Jean leaned forward to me smiling and said, very softly, 'She can be a terrorist sometimes, can't she?'

To my horror a tear welled up and I dabbed at it with the back of my hand. 'Oh, God,' I said, put the champagne down and buried my face in my hands. 'Oh, God,' I muttered through wet fingers. There was a short atrocious silence, and then there were comforting hands on my shoulders. They were Natasha's. I shook her off angrily and sat up straight. She sat down again, and I could see that she was hurt. Then she took Jean's arm in hers, and leaned against her, reminding me insistently of her new possession.

'No,' I said, more firmly. 'I should tell you.' There was a sudden chorus of movement from Jean and Natasha, shrugged disclaimers of no obligation, their hands frantically signalling their lack of interest in mere gossip. But it was my turn to insist: 'No, no, I want to tell you. It will do me good.'

Jean filled our glasses again, and I began my short and simple tale. 'Teboso is Teboso Ngqayimbana,' I said to Jean, by way of introducing it.

Her hand went up to her mouth. 'A native?' she asked, dismayed.

'Yes, a native. He's my garden boy.'

Jean looked puzzled. 'Your garden boy? But does this flat have a garden?'

I ignored her and said, 'I was with him just now. He wanted to screw me. I just got back when you came in.'

'Well,' asked Natasha — can you say that a voice gleams with excitement? — 'did you?'

I downed half my champagne; I was beginning to shake, perhaps the after-effects of strong emotion, or perhaps it was physical exertion I wasn't used to. 'Sort of,' I replied.

'With a *garden boy*?' asked Jean softly, as if stunned, disbelieving. Her hand was still held to her mouth.

'What do you mean "sort of"?' demanded Natasha. 'I mean, either you screwed him or you didn't, surely!'

'No, just sort of.' Despite my attempt at boldness, I had turned completely scarlet. I had the rest of the champagne. It didn't help at all. I held out my glass for more. Jean tried but the last drops trickled out of the mouth of the bottle.

'I just — he — everything except — I wouldn't let him penetrate.'

'So? What's the big deal?' Natasha exclaimed. 'Why should you let him penetrate anyway?'

'Exactly,' I said. 'We had a fight about it.'

'Oh, God,' they both said, 'just like a man.'

'Just like a man,' repeated Natasha, this time on her own. 'They make a mess all around you with their socks and their newspapers, and then they want to leave their mess inside you too.'

'Of course I told him to get out of my life. Or I sort of suggested it, anyway.'

'Of course,' they said indignantly. 'There's a limit to hospitality,' added Natasha.

'But I don't want him to. That's the problem.'

Natasha naturally had no problem at all. 'I am sure,' she pronounced, 'that he will realise before the end that it's all rhetoric. He'll come round, you'll see.' What she meant by all rhetoric I still don't know.

I didn't tell them what really hurt: Teboso saying, tiredly, quite gently really, a world of self-admiring critique in a sentence: 'Little European Bo Peep: go home.' And I had walked out without adding a word more, leaving the door open. And I didn't tell them why I wouldn't let him penetrate my body, knowing they wouldn't think an explanation necessary.

Natasha threaded her fingers through Jean's and said, 'Well, at least I'm alright.' It was the most inane, ill-timed thing I'd ever heard her say, but I held my tongue.

5

For a while I was mired in anger and self-doubt. To make matters worse, Teboso phoned me and invited me to a party in Guguletu. An American student,

Amy Biehl, had been murdered in one of the black slums a few years before. I was painfully apprehensive of the danger.

I was filled with as much guilt as fear. I said, 'No, Teboso. I can't.' And then a second fear, this time of rejection: white guilt raging.

I heard him breathing down the line. Then: 'You don't want to come into Guguletu.'

'It could be pretty dangerous for me.'

'That is not a statement without properties, Jessica. We could examine it, you know. It is not lacking in political content. What, for example, do you mean by "dangerous"? There are many kinds of danger. There are many kinds of dangerous encounter.'

Was he angry? The line between us stretched taut. 'Teboso, can't you see what I'm saying? This is very simple! Simple physical danger! You can't pretend it's not there. I have no other objection to going into Guguletu.'

'Let us bring our minds to bear, let us examine this thing, Jessica. What do you mean by "no other objection"? Why do you structure your communication in that particular way?'

'Teboso, what is going on? What game are you playing? If you're angry, just say so for God's sake.'

He spoke slowly: 'Jessica. Jessica. The last thing I am is angry. I just want to know what you mean when you express yourself as you do. Let us unpack your words and look at your meanings, that is all I am saying.'

I slammed the phone down.

About two days later he phoned me again as if nothing had happened, and calmly invited me to an ANC fundraiser. 'This might be more to your taste,' he said. 'It's at the Western Province Cricket Club. In Newlands, not Guguletu. Next Sunday. I don't think anyone's been murdered there for a while.' I dithered, and he said: 'Nor do I think the Claremont branch of the ANC will slaughter an ox there and put blood on the carpet.' I accepted, dropped the phone and cursed myself in foul and sustained terms for exposing myself to him further.

It was my day for being abused. As I settled down to work on an assignment, the bell rang. It was Natasha. She invited herself in to 'touch base'. I glanced at my watch and let her in. We sat down, and she pulled her chair so far forward that our knees were uncomfortably close. She said, 'Jessica, we've known each other a long time.'

I agreed.

'We are *extremely* good friends.'

I agreed to that too.

'That means we can say just about anything we like to each other.'

'I'm not sure if I agree with that part entirely ...'

'You know what I mean, Jessica. I mean we can be utterly *honest* with each other, don't you think so?' Before I could reply she said, 'I've been very worried about you, darling. And I just have to clear the air. Because really, you are my friend and I can no longer stand back and let this all happen without saying anything.'

'Let what happen? What?'

She hitched her chair even closer — our knees were touching now — and related everything that was wrong with me: I probably didn't realise it, but all my friends were concerned about this *incredible trip* I was on. I had become so prickly and narcissistic that I was just about *impossible* to be with. Not to mention volatile and moody. I had become judgemental and threatening and superior to everyone who came across me. It was a case of *radical chic* at its worst!

'Jesus, Goldman,' I protested. 'All my friends. You've consulted my friends and they all agree with you. You're all theatre critics, every single person I know, and you've all got the right to comment on my life —'

She stopped me with a gesture and said: 'No need to defend yourself against *moi*, of course not. I'm the one who understands.'

'But Natasha, what do you understand? How come you understand when I don't know what you're talking about!'

She stopped dead. Then, in dowager accents: 'You mean to tell me that you honestly and sincerely don't know what I'm referring to? It's your black lover, my dear. It has gone *straight* to your head!'

I put my head in my hands. I peered through my fingers to see if she was still there. I saw a maddeningly smug face. A fatuous one too: Teboso and I could hardly be called lovers.

'Natasha,' I said. 'Thank you for sharing this with me.'

She spread her hand out on her breast self-deprecatingly and said, 'I only do this because I care so much about you, darling.'

Teboso drove badly. If he saw anything red — brake lights, traffic lights, stop streets — he accelerated and then braked at the last minute. After being thrown about in his Opel, it was a relief to stop at the WP Cricket Club in Newlands. I glanced at him as we crossed the threshold. His face was completely unreadable.

We were late, it was crowded inside and serious inroads had been made at the bar tables. Cyril Ramaphosa was holding the floor. It was the first time I had seen him live. His urbane phrases rolled out, his comfortable laughter. He was just killing time, he explained frankly, because Evita Bezuidenhout was late. But he did so with sublime ease. Just to his right Kader Asmal puffed away at a cigarette. I caught sight of Chris Ball, and recognised the poet Tatamkhulu Afrika, and the bearded professor of literature who appeared in Vodacom ads, and the singer David Kramer and the publisher-poet Gus Ferguson.

'This is like a newspaper,' I whispered to Teboso. 'Being inside one, I mean.'

He smiled at me in a very grown-up way.

A tall woman wearing an evening gown and a dense black honeycomb wig drifted past me. There was something eerie about her passage. Then I recognised her as the famous drag artist Evita Bezuidenhout. She made her way to the podium.

Ramaphosa stopped, turned and welcomed this new arrival. The applause was thunderous as she climbed up, ungainly on her stilettos. Her well-tried patter poured out, the old jokes about Nationalists and Afrikaners and the New South Africa, her trademark Pretoria accent. 'Don't I recognise some of you?' she asked her audience. 'Didn't I see you all at the Democratic Party congress a few years ago?' The laughter ratcheted up the register of unease, new layers of hysteria added. 'I don't see many people from Khayelitsha here.' Then she turned directly to Teboso and said, 'Are you the token black?'

Teboso cracked up. He laughed till his eyes ran. He took off his spectacles and wiped his eyes and laughed some more. When he put them on again, the light fell across opaque patches of grease, whether from his tears or the snacks he had handled, I couldn't say. I stared at him: his chubby face monumental after the dissolution of laughter, coarse-grained, the lenses of his spectacles smudged. The image seemed to measure his mass for me, his personal gravity. I felt insubstantial compared to him — too neb-ulous, too white, too loosely anchored in the world.

Later that evening, many drinks later, he asked, 'Why are you so crestfallen, Jessica?'

'I am not crestfallen,' I objected. 'Why describe me in such terms? What do you get out of it?'

He put his arm around me in a grand paternalistic hug, and said, 'Jessica, Jessica,' in a gravelly sing-song voice, tired and bored and amused at once. 'You need to live more, that's all. Time is on your side.'

I swore at him under my breath, and walked off. I don't think he noticed any significance in this departure. I might have been going to refill my glass, or to the loo. I walked on out of the lounge venue, out the lobby and down the steps. It was cold outside, the air burnt by the stink of exhaust fumes. The overcast sky was tinged a sick orange by the lights of the city. I tasted metal on my tongue. I walked home, though it was a stupid and dangerous thing to do.

6

On the weekend, Teboso accompanied me to Franschhoek. I concentrated on driving. He concentrated on an academic paper he was editing. As we passed three dead trees clawing their way out of a waterhole, he said: 'But do you agree with Fanon?'

'Who? Never heard of him.' He buried his head in the paper again. After I while I asked, 'What about Fanon?'

He looked up, startled: 'I never said anything about Fanon.'

I smiled at him.

We reached the railway bridge over the Berg River. As the car bucked along the sleepers, Teboso pursed his lips and began whistling 'Eine kleine Nachtmusik'. He was slightly flat and varied his tempo, setting my teeth on edge. He interrupted himself and asked: 'You did say we're going to your uncle? Koos? Koen?'

'Koen,' I said. 'No, we're not. I don't want to see him just yet.'

The truth was that I didn't want Koen to see Teboso just yet. God alone knew what kind of embarrassment might result from that encounter.

'Okay. No Uncle Koos. Where are we going then?'

'My grandparents' house. I need to see the place.'

'Ah, your roots, Jessica, your roots.'

He said it with such meaty pleasure that I coloured.

He added: 'Three generations in the country. You are a complete African.' Before I could react, he looked at me slyly and said, 'General Constand Viljoen is an African. Mr FW De Klerk is an African. We only have Africans in this country.'

'But some are more African than others?'

He pretended to read his article. I was learning that Teboso never gave a point away.

The house was a large, rambling Victorian — in any event, what passes in South African towns as Victorian — with a great deal of porch and cast-iron ornamentation on the gutters and posts, too many rooms collected under a tin roof — in all, an agreeable hulk. The house was dilapidated, the plot large and untidy, distinguished by a stream running diagonally through it, and ancient fruit trees. Hens clucked in the garden, and the flat protest of ducks sounded from behind the house.

I rang the doorbell, heard chimes in the interior. Hesitant footsteps approached. An old woman opened the door only a few inches and peered at us. 'Yes?' she enquired, her single word bearing the same freight of suspicion and anxiety as her cornflower blue eyes.

'I'm Jessica Kruger,' I said, sticking out my hand. 'I hope this isn't inconvenient. My grandparents used to live here, and I was hoping to see the house.' She ignored my hand. 'If you don't mind,' I added lamely.

'Kruger, you say. Yes, that's right. The Krugers had to move out when we bought the house.' Then with a frail smile: 'That was a long time ago of course.' Her glance shifted to Teboso and back. 'They were nice people. But that was a very long time ago, long before you were born in fact.'

'Would you mind terribly much if we came in and had a look round?'

'Are they still alive then? Your grandparents?'

'My grandmother is alive and well. My grandfather died some years ago.'

She seemed to consider this, then said: 'She must be very nearly as old as me.' Her frail smile again: 'That is very old, you know. Far too old.'

'Not at all,' I said, trying to produce the inanities about

age that age requires. I failed. Teboso sighed. 'Would you mind,' I asked, 'if we came in and had a look at the house? If it's not too invasive?'

'I don't mind,' she said, without enthusiasm. She surrendered control of the door and stood back. As we approached, she remarked, 'I think your boy must stay outside. Your driver.'

I stopped dead, and turned to face Teboso. He said, 'Madam must go in. I will wait outside for Nkosana.'

I turned back to the old woman. She hovered before me, a wrinkled face in a doorway, painted there, live with reference to other faces like it, all forbidding and secretive. I swung back to Teboso and saw light flashing off thick lenses. Below it, his tight demonic smile. I knew I couldn't go in.

'I'm sorry,' I said, 'I think we'll go.'

Her face seemed to slacken. It was her only enquiry. I pointed to Teboso — my skin blazed — 'he's not my driver, and if he can't come in —'

'Well suit yourself,' she said, 'though why you come knocking on my door I don't know.'

Before I could offer further confused protestation, the owner of my grandparents' house shuffled back and closed the door on us, leaving a scent of Pears soap behind her. Over the rattling of her security chain I heard her last words: 'You don't seem to know what you want. Wasting my time like this, it's very rude.'

'Let us read this as a myth,' said Teboso. 'A dream, if you like. Consider: you cannot enter the house of your ancestors. There is a guardian at the door, the old woman. She knows your grandparents, but only the autologous in blood may enter her lodge. You know, the right clan. Now you are in the middle, you Jessica. This house holds the secrets of your past. But you cannot go in because you have to leave your kaffir boy behind. Your so-called driver, but really your shadow, your dark secret. You won't do this, you won't go in. Why not? Not because you are too attached to this horse of another colour, but because you are a liberal. You are simply too well-meaning and politically virtuous to go in alone.'

'Teboso, how can you say that?'

'However,' he said, ignoring my objection, 'you need to go in. Unless you go in, you will never learn the secrets of your own soul. You will never confront the origins of your psyche. That is your dilemma.'

As I drove, I found myself weighing my options. I refused for once to react blindly.

He sailed on: 'Paradoxically, it is not my darkness that keeps you outside. It is your precious world of light. If you followed the instinct of blood, of darkness, you would simply go in.'

'Leaving you outside?'

'Of course. That is what I would have done. I will even say: that is what you should have done.'

I just drove. I felt mute. Resentment flamed through my body. I was literally mute too. Why did he think I was a liberal? I didn't even know what a liberal was, really, other than someone who voted for the Democratic Party as my parents did, and had pronounced political views that corresponded roughly with being English, which my parents weren't.

At first I thought he was whistling. But in fact he was laughing silently. I glanced sideways and saw his belly quaking under the seatbelt.

'I am the token black,' he said softly. Then he let out a great breath, as if the matter had been dealt with and could be left alone. His smile was angelic now, snidely angelic. 'What do you say, Jessica?'

I let the car slow to a crawl, and guided it to the verge of the road. I was too upset to drive. I gripped the wheel and felt the old woman's face staring out of my own. So be it, I thought: my own chill blood. Let it speak. I heard my voice, thin and vinegar with anger: 'I am tired of your condescension, Teboso. I am tired of your paternalism.'

He was taken aback. '*My* condescension? *My* paternalism?'

Then I was swamped by rage. 'Do I have to earn my Africanness? Who decides who qualifies to be an African? Is that your privilege? Are you the judge? What, are you going to stick a pencil through my hair?'

He remained hatefully calm. 'Consider, Jessica. Consider. What is Franschhoek?'

'What do you mean "what is Franschhoek"? It's a town, that's all.'

'No, Jessica, no. Let us unpack this thing you think is a town. It is more than a town. That phenomenon of Franschhoek, that thing you call Franschhoek, it is a European colonial settlement. It is not just a town.'

I suddenly realised that he wasn't as dispassionate as he pretended to be. His dialect and accent had thickened.

He was pointing his stubby finger at me: 'What you call Franschhoek projects a certain order onto this world — this indigenous world, this place where the ignorant savages like myself run about in the bush. Now what are the characteristics of this special order? Its one chief characteristic is a blindness. It's a *blindness*. The owner of that house — she does not want to let me in. What does this mean? She does not want to see me in her house. She wants to suppress me from consciousness.'

Despite my anger, I had to smile. 'Chrissake, how can you identify me with that woman? What have I got to do with Franschhoek anyway? Why bring it up at all?'

He was plainly agitated at last. 'You are a Franschhoek! — yes, you. I mean it. You are that old woman. You won't let me in, not even surrounded with rubber. Have you even once felt my live black prick in your European vagina?'

I looked at him in the most complete astonishment. 'Why, Teboso! What on earth has that go to do with anything —' Then my anger drained away as it dawned on me: 'Teboso,' I said, 'are you trying to tell me that anything I do matters to you?'

He cleared his throat and stared straight ahead.

'Even if only as a sexual curiosity?'

He cleared his throat again, an abrupt, dignified grunt.

'Or maybe as an incomplete conquest — a horribly extended coitus interruptus?'

Silence. Then that grunt again. How could this short guttural sound hold such reserves of sullen strangling manhood?

I reached for his belt. As I unbuckled it and undid his fly, I said, 'Or are you just the teensiest bit hurt? You know, that I don't love you enough?'

He opened his mouth to say something, but never quite got it out. His lips remained parted, plump and dark.

When he was aroused to my satisfaction I flicked his member and said, 'Now that's an ignorant savage stuck in the bush.'

I left him as he was, put the car into gear and lurched back onto the road.

'Bitch,' he said softly.

We drove on to Cape Town. I felt giddy, with alarm at my presumption and with fear too — of the unbreakable silence which enveloped us, of the rage emanating silently from him.

7

My parents had arrived unexpectedly in Cape Town. My father was here for a physics conference. As I drove to their hotel, I was pleased and yet apprehensive.

My mother was waiting for me in the lobby. She didn't recognise me at first.

'Aretha!' I called. She swung about myopically, then found me. We ran at each other, exchanging squeals of delight, and hugged each other.

'Jessica! Oh, my darling, it's so nice to see you!' She held me at arm's length and inspected me. 'You've filled out.'

'I've picked up weight!'

'No, not at all. You've absolutely filled out. I think you look more womanly, yes, that's it, but something else has changed.'

'No it hasn't,' I said breathlessly. 'Where's Sybrand? Conferencing, I suppose?'

When my mother and I are together, our speech tends to accelerate and our sentences blur together. My father once called it 'a process of mutual verbal liquefaction'. This meeting was no exception, and we rattled on giddily. We ensconced ourselves on the verandah, and laced with jam and scones and strong potions of Earl Grey tea, our loquacity might even have steepened. Yet despite the odds against it happening at all, there was a lull in our conversation, marked by the gentile clashing of hotel silver and the hushed passage of waiters.

Breaking it, my mother remarked, 'No, I insist you have changed, at least a little. You're more substantial.'

'Do you have to harp on my weight? I haven't gained that much.'

Aretha looked into the middle distance. When her eyes went watery and vague, I know she would be hunting something particular.

'Did you know,' she said, 'that the tea plant absorbs aluminium salts from the soil? That's why we think that Asians are inscrutable. Half of them probably have Alzheimer's.'

'Probably,' I agreed. 'It would explain the English too.'

But her misdirection went only so far, then suddenly swerved back on track: 'No, Jessica, I'm sure it's the soul.' She was referring to mine. 'A sea change, I have no doubt.'

I felt my mouth pulling its wryest smile. I said, 'I have a new boyfriend.'

My mother blinked.

'His name is Teboso Ngqayimbana.'

She blinked again. I think she turned pale; perhaps it was

the watery light of late afternoon.

'Look on the bright side, Aretha. At least I'm not sitting here telling you I'm gay.'

This time she didn't even blink. Then slowly, slowly, she resumed breathing.

'Teboso who?'

'Ngqayimbana.'

She repeated it accurately. Then: 'This is a little bit of a shock, Jessica, as you might imagine. Why didn't you tell us before?'

'I'm telling you now,' I replied patiently.

'But to wait till we're here and spring this on us —'

'It would be a shock under any conditions,' I said.

She turned scarlet, as I do, and placed her hand on mine.

'I'm so embarrassed, my darling, by my own reaction. But this is difficult for me.'

'I know,' I replied. 'You're a liberal.'

I regretted my glib little cruelty. But I also felt defiant in advance, once my love was exposed: tangled in a thicket of social unease. I thought of all the pretending everyone would have to do and wanted to die, of sheer boredom.

My father had been forewarned and so put a better face on things. When we ate together that night, he brought up the topic as neutrally as possible. It was a measure of his restraint that this happened only over coffee. 'I'm eager to meet your new boyfriend,' he said. 'Do you think we could set up a meeting? I'm free on Wednesday night, if that would suit everyone else. We could eat out.'

'Sure,' I replied noncommittally. 'I'll check with Teboso.'

I glanced covertly at my mother, trying to read from her what had passed between them. I read only new dimensions of anxiety and care. AIDS, said her face. Cultural differences. Extremes of chauvinism. Nothing I hadn't thought about myself, long and hard. She would have added mixed-race children to the list, no doubt. I decided to look elsewhere. My father's face had set in a quizzical mask well before I knew him, a rigor of permanent enquiry which many people mistook for simple angst. But his expression was now strained into such a tortured form of itself that I had to smile.

'You're laughing at me,' he complained gently.

'You're a cartoon sometimes, Sybrand.' To soften my helpless sharpness, I added, 'I'm uneasy, Dad. I just don't know what Teboso will say when he meets you. He's like a savage running around in the bush.'

'Really?' exclaimed my mother.

'Really. That's exactly what he is. And I'm not sure you can call him my boyfriend either. He's far too unpredictable for that.'

My parents exchanged glances, but didn't dare probe further. My father permitted himself one tart comment: 'Well, you're so predictable yourself, it must be a marriage made in heaven.'

I had to screw up my nerve to invite Teboso to this meal. I knew he would still be angry with me, and we hadn't communicated since that disastrous trip to Franschhoek. I still felt guilty about the way I had treated him, wondering what on earth had possessed me to play with his dignity so flippantly. As always, he was short and unreadable on the phone, and the last thing I knew was where I stood. To make matters worse, I had chosen the Silver Dragon Chinese Restaurant, the site of our first meal.

Teboso was about forty minutes late. No one said anything about it, but as we worked our way down the bottle of white wine, something ugly, derisive, stamped itself into the air above the table like an invisible motto: 'African time'.

'Ah, at last,' said my father, raising his head and turning towards the entrance, 'This must be Teboso.' As we followed his gaze, I tried to see things through my parents' eyes: a portly African walking unhurriedly towards us, his face impassive, unreadable behind thick spectacles, his lips drawn into a plump, pensive bow.

Then there was my mother's wide smile. She smiles very widely when she's tense, and becomes too animated. Verging on silly, I think. 'Oh, Teboso,' she exclaimed, 'I am so very glad to meet you.'

He shook her hand and said, 'Uh-huh,' with his customary finesse.

'Hullo, Teboso,' said my father, his manner more easy than my mother, though he managed to imply by his tone that he was a person of considerable importance. 'Sybrand Kruger, and this is my wife Aretha. I need hardly introduce you to Jessica.'

Teboso sat down opposite me without apologising for his lateness. Then he looked round the table and said, 'How do you do,' to no-one in particular. He turned to me and nodded, as if to some faint acquaintance. Without transition, without warning, I was bright scarlet.

In the silence that followed, I suffered the sudden intense fantasy that this was a painting. We were stuck in our positions for ever. Our expressions would never change. Two anxious white faces, one dark and round, one hysterical and red. We might have been hanging in the Irma Stern Museum.

My mother broke it: 'Well then, everyone, what shall we order?' My father picked up Teboso's inverted glass, turned it the right way up and filled it, without asking him. Teboso raised the glass, cleared his throat and said, 'Chin-chin.' We all looked at him in surprise.

The meal was not a tremendous success. Teboso remained taciturn and irritable. My parents were amiable at first — 'well meaning,' Teboso might have said — then as they felt rebuffed, increasingly brittle. He managed to fit in his joke about being the token black, but this time sounded bitter and callow.

I grew alarmingly clear-headed, as if one could tear away the skin of this meeting and inspect bare bones, map in stark detail the position that each of us really occupied. Our speech grew dull and distant, and through the chiming of forks and glasses I heard a colder, more real language.

I find your daughter interesting, Teboso might have told my parents. An exotic fruit worth unpeeling, though it's taking far more time than I would think necessary. But there is no future in it, and I don't want to waste my time on her attachments, peripheral figures such as yourselves.

Mr Ngqayimbana, said Aretha, you are a terrible threat to my daughter. I find you dark and wild and angry. Your egotism appals me and I cannot guess what diseases you bear in your blood. Perhaps the affront of your presence can be overcome in time, but I shall never forgive you for this: you are an even greater threat to my vision of Africa and my own place in it.

Sybrand turned to me and said: My dearest Jessica, you force me to admire your willingness to explore, and I acknowledge your freedom to do so. But I am angry, deeply angry, at my own ambivalence towards your black lover. I am angry with him for using you so charmlessly. And I am angry with you for doing this to me. I have large and important projects to manage, and I need things to run more smoothly in my family.

On the surface, things proceeded dully enough. My mother questioned Teboso about his interests; my father and Teboso discussed the politics of research funding and found common ground. I confined myself to comments on the food, retreating from a situation that made me tense. I wasn't at peace with my ancestors, but I had heard their voices. And what did I say to them? If I did say anything clearly, it could have been this: I stagger under the burden of guilt I carry, the guilt of false premises. Everything you've said tonight is half mistaken. Ngqayimbana is barely my lover and partly my enemy. He remains alien, as you need him to be, something I desire and reject at once.

Now what did Teboso say to me? Something very simple: what are you playing at, Jessica? Why do you toy with me sexually? And even in this secret impersonal language I was busy discovering, I withheld the answer. It was too embarrassing a thing to mention in polite society.

Sound might have blurred. The banal wash of conversation resumed, bringing with it restaurant noise and the usual static of personal concealment. Teboso lifted a thimble of green tea to his lips, slurped audibly, and said, 'Did you know that Rudolf Steiner regarded Chinese culture as a stagnant remnant of the Atlantean?'

My father lifted his eyebrows. 'Come now. Atlantean? Do you mean to tell me you believe in Atlantis?'

Embarrassment washed over me.

'It is not a question of what I believe,' Teboso replied. 'It is a question of a contemporary myth that is widely subscribed to. We all seem to need a golden age, however lost it might be.' He launched into a discourse on what various authors had written on the subject.

My father's face tightened into a mask of scepticism. His forefinger was tapping on the table rapidly as Teboso spoke. His eyes were bloodshot, and in this dim light, I suddenly thought him very ugly. As he reached for his cup of tea, the little vessel shattered. His hand jerked back, stung.

As the fuss my mother made over the incident reached its crescendo and died away, I saw Teboso watching me, musing. Then he pointed at my father, and said, 'I don't suppose you'll believe this either, Sybrand, if I tell you that your daughter is something of a poltergeist.'

We all stared at him. Then my father's face crumpled into laughter. He laughed until he wept. Teboso retreated into the same glacial silence I had experienced on the road from Franschhoek.

8

Teboso didn't contact me for some time. I tried phoning him, but could only reach his answering machine. He didn't return my calls. I still attended his lectures though. We pretended we were nothing to each other. I pretended he was an advanced answering machine, one capable of spouting out anthropology. Then I stopped going to his classes. I was damned if I would go to his office.

I swallowed my pride eventually, went to his flat and rang the bell. Chill wind in the open corridor, bruised clouds above, the sky darkening. There were lights on in the flat, but no response. Had he seen me approach? Was he there or not? I left, angry with him, and even more angry with myself for exposing myself to this kind of humiliation. His car was parked in the street, in its usual place.

I walked down the streets of Observatory, not exactly heedless of the risk but too enraged to care. The tiny gardens were jagged with leaves that shone dully, black in sodium streetlight. Yellow light spilled out of windows, excluding me from whatever their interiors promised.

I ate alone in a near-empty pizza joint. The food tasted of ash. I went back to my flat. I had never realised before that the parquet flooring was so hard and cold, or that footsteps could be so audible.

I was driven out by the resonant silence of my flat. I drove to Natasha's townhouse in Camps Bay and pressed the intercom.

She let me in. 'You look grey, darling,' she said. 'Don't tell me, I know — man wasn't meant to be alone. Woman neither.'

'Is Jean with you?'

'Oh, God no. I turfed her out. I don't mind the Portuguese, and I don't mind the Roman Catholic. But the *petit bourgeois* gets a bit much.'

Why is nothing easy, I asked myself. Why is everything concealed under layers of theatre paint? To my mind, her expression was tragic, if university students can ever be considered tragic. Beneath her buoyant young flesh I saw an older woman looking out, a sad and weary face almost filtered out by the mask of youth. But I knew and felt that she was offering me a home, if only for a weekend or part of that, and I knew that she had no need to question my good faith.

'Doing anything?'

'Me, Jessica? Doing? Don't you know that if you come knocking on my door, which hardly ever happens, I will put aside immediately whatever trivial thing I happen to be wasting my time on and give you my complete attention?'

'I wouldn't expect anything less,' I replied, and entered.

We walked down the beach. The light had decayed to old gold, the water was turquoise. If you kick sand on the beach at Camps Bay with the ball of your foot, it squeaks cleanly, as if alive.

She took my hand. I didn't really mind. 'We don't talk anymore, Jessica. We only swop — what do you call them? Soundbites.'

'What would you like to talk about?'

'You know what I would like to talk about. You and Teboso whatsisname.'

We walked on. I made my feet squeak on the sand.

'I need to go down to the water,' I said.

We stood in the Atlantic surge, sinking ankle-deep into the soft, bitterly cold mud.

'It hurts,' I said, talking about the water, but thinking about Teboso. 'It hurts to the bone.'

'Why are we standing here then?'

'I need to hurt —'

She led me back to the dry sand, and we sat down facing the sea. Her hand rested lightly on the inside of my thigh. I paid it no particular attention.

'You talk of my black lover. You talk of radical chic. My parents are going quietly berserk. So quietly that they don't even know it. But it's all so excessive and — oh, I don't know. Out of place.'

'What, Jessica, what? What is out of place?'

'Your basic understanding of the situation. You've all got it wrong: I haven't let him fuck me yet.'

'Well, why not? Why don't you just fuck him so that we can all understand the situation correctly?'

I lifted her hand off my leg and turned it upwards, holding it in both of mine. I inspected her palm in what was left of the light. The human hand is an impossible device.

I released it — it drifted back to my thigh — stared down at the sand and replied, 'Because I'm still a virgin.'

There was a terribly long silence. I was shivering by now, at the mercy of frigid air moving slowly off the sea.

'Look at me, Jessica,' said Natasha. I looked at her. 'Would you like me to do something about it? It will be easier with a woman.'

I shook my head.

'Your lips are blue,' she said. She leant forward and kissed me — her tongue entered my mouth — I jerked back. 'Poor thing,' she said. 'It's all so complicated when you're a virgin.'

I breathed slowly through the mauve taste of her flesh inside my own.

'It stays that way,' she said. 'When you're not a virgin it's just as complicated. There's no way out.'

She took me out to supper. We ate at a Turkish restaurant in Greenpoint. Halfway through the meal I woke up to the subtle shift that had taken place.

'Natasha,' I said, 'this is just like you're dating me!'

It was very loud in the restaurant and she pretended not to hear me. 'Your manners,' I said, 'normally you don't have any. Tonight you even opened the car door for me. And pouring my wine and deferring to my choices ... I've been feeling like an honoured guest without knowing why.'

'What? What did you say?'

'I predict you're going to insist on paying.'

She kept up her charade of deafness.

'It's okay, Natasha,' I said. 'This is exactly what I need: a good massage for my ego.'

'Darling,' she said eventually, 'you're far too clever for little old me.' She put on her Police sunglasses. She sat before me with her raven hair and little round blue shades in this cavernous, dimly lit interior, plumper than she had been at the beginning of the year, a compromised smile on her face, and stuck a cigarette in her mouth. 'Oh, God,' she said. 'Caught out again.'

I felt a terrible surge of love for her. It was wonderful to feel love so simply. To be allowed to love.

In the early hours of the morning I was woken by a growing nausea. I barely made it to the toilet. The sound of my retching woke Natasha and when I returned to bed she was sitting up naked. I was struck at once by the beauty of her overfull breasts, her rounded shoulders, and by her expression of despondency. The weariness and age I had seen hidden in her face only hours before surfaced fully now.

'You're vomiting because you've been in my bed,' she said.

'That's totally unreasonable, Natasha!' I exclaimed. 'How can you say that? It's the food, the rich food. Something I ate, that's all there is to it. So what if I slept in your bed! It's the only bed in the flat, isn't it?'

I flopped back, exasperated as well as nauseous. 'Well I'm not sleeping on the floor,' I said, 'even if you think your bed has something to do with this.'

'Well then, I'll sleep on the floor,' she replied. She started up.

'Goldman,' I said irritably, 'Schmalz like this I don't need.'

She collapsed back onto her cushion and sulked.

I woke up late. I didn't know where I was, or why I felt disorientated. Slowly, slowly, everything came back. I stared at the ceiling for a long time, inhaling the unfamiliar scents of someone else's bed, absorbing the mood of Natasha's terracotta room. I was no longer ill, but I felt weak, and my stomach muscles were sore.

She had gone out, leaving a note for me in the kitchen, next to the kettle. It said simply, 'You've broken my sunglasses.'

'Nonsense, Goldman,' I said aloud. 'I never touched your glasses.'

Then I saw the Police spectacles lying on the counter. I picked them up and turned them over in astonishment. One of the lenses was cracked across the centre. Perhaps Teboso was right. Perhaps I was a poltergeist, a malicious spirit that breaks things without intending to, knowing no other lore. Perhaps this was another of Natasha's strange suppositions. I put down the sunglasses carefully.

I opened a tin of pilchards. I broke one of the fish taking it out. A part of its spine jutted out, stained sepia. The meat was sepia. The skin glinted. I couldn't eat it. I picked up the tin by its lid and dropped it in the bin.

I drove through the evening traffic to Ngqayimbana's flat, wondering what I should say. Fragments of greeting, broken sentences, excuses, explanations of motive, lies. I cursed myself for going there at all.

He came to the door and looked at me as if I were selling vacuum cleaners. He said nothing, presented only an indifferent look of enquiry.

'Teboso,' I said. 'I need to speak to you.'

The same blank look.

A sense of futility stopped me in my tracks. 'Sorry,' I said, 'this is a waste of time. Shouldn't have come.'

A slow dawning of surprise was the only change in his expression. I turned to go. He said, 'Wait, Jessica, wait a minute.'

I turned back. He seemed to look past my shoulder for an embarrassing length of time.

'What, Teboso, what?'

'You won't settle down in my mind.'

'What's that supposed to mean?'

He was still looking at the wall behind me. 'Ah, if I must

be frank with you, Jessica, I would say that you won't settle down in my mind.'

'Well, that's great. That's exactly what I came here to hear.'

'No, you mustn't take offence at my feedback. I am trying to be objective, insofar as this is possible. I do not regard objectivity as, you know, the holy grail. But I am just trying to tell you an aspect of things.'

Every life-supporting instinct told me to walk away. I said, 'What are you trying to tell me, Teboso? Please explain yourself clearly and simply so that a limited being such as a woman can understand.

'I mean exactly what I said. There is something juvenile about you that doesn't gel with your age. You won't settle down in my mind, that's all.'

'Something *juvenile*?' The word wouldn't die away. My rage soared.

'You must focus yourself, you know. You must decide what you are. You must decide what you want. Then you must take what you want. Then you must live with what you take. This is elementary, Jessica. Please speak to me again when, you know, you have worked some of this out.'

He looked at me fully for the first time. His eyes were tightly intelligent, his lips plump and firm and righteous.

'Jesus, Teboso,' I said. 'Aren't you just the wisest thing I've ever come across?'

He looked at me even more righteously.

I shook my head at him in disbelief, and laughed. 'I won't even attempt, Teboso, to describe you — you know, to yourself. As I see you —'

He closed the door on me, with great dignity. I kicked it so hard it shuddered in the frame — easy when you're wearing Doc Martens — and walked off.

I did something I never do, and wrote to my mother:

Dear Aretha

You'll be relieved to hear that my relationship with Teboso proba-bly won't go much further. After several abortive attempts to con-tact him, I've come to realise that he is just toying with me. He is either never available, or when he is, plays at being the master of universal wisdom. I know he is older than me and I respect the fact that he knows more about life than I do, but I can only take so much condescension, so much arrogance, so much masterly reticence. I've decided to stop being grist for the mill of his ego — yes, I think he sees me as a very ordinary person, even a dull one, the ideal butt for sharpening his wit on. I'm not sure if I've mixed metaphors there or even if it's grammatical, but at the moment I'm too angry to care about things like grammar.

My work is mostly up to scratch, except for one particular project, but I'm getting very frustrated with things, and I find nothing more exhausting than a state of sustained anger. I would probably only admit it to you, but losing Teboso hurts. That is, if I have lost him. And not knowing hurts too. I feel very hemmed in by things, by faces, blank faces, doors in my face.

After I signed it, I tore up the letter and threw the frag-ments away. I was too angry with my parents to send them such a confession. Part of the anger was about Teboso. I did want him, I did like him, and that infuriated me even more.

9

I resumed my much interrupted history project. This time I thought I would concentrate on Jolene Galant. I dug up the photograph my mother had sent of her, bearing (of all things) a coffee tray. Who are you, I thought, what did you get up to with my grandfather?

I cut lectures on Friday and drove out to Pniel. The hamlet is so small that one could probably walk round it in half an hour. Small, mostly well-kept houses. Fruit trees everywhere, plane trees and oak — a kind of deciduous rain forest — and dazzling zinc roofs reflecting the sun. A Dutch Reformed church dominated the village, with small proud obelisks jutting up on either side of the gable. The bell, like a slave bell, supported by two rectangular columns about eight feet high. In a rough piazza opposite the church, there was a strange fountain consisting of a pair of stylised doves, about a metre high. I thought they had been hammered out of two sheets of scrap aluminium. A galvanised pipe stuck up from between them, surmounted by an ordinary shower head. The fountain was dry.

There was a river below the town, clean water running through rounded ochre stones, and beautiful trees crowding its course. As I walked by I wanted to sink into that water, to let it wash over my soul like a concentrate of the clean and simple world I imagined Pniel to be. But there were three boys sunning themselves where I passed by, naked from the waist up, their bodies soaking up sunlight like phototropic plants, and I knew I couldn't unclothe myself in their presence. We looked at each other suspiciously — I had the feeling that they weren't here in my own time at all — I wanted to ask them if they knew Jolene Galant, a girl about their age, and where she lived.

I fetched up back at the church. There was a plaque under the bell that read:

OPGERIG OP 17 APRIL 1938
IN DANKBARE HERINNERING
AAN
EERW J.F. STEGMANN
STIGTER VAN HIERDIE GEMEENTE
IN DIE JAAR 1843

My rather crumpled photograph of Jolene Galant had been taken the year before the consecration of the church. I squinted up at that stolid building as if it might contain her secrets. The plaster of the façade was uneven, and so was rouged in places with shadow. This play of light emphasised the texture. Something about it suggested a human face, one chiselled of stone so subtly that the nuances of flesh were created. But not cold flesh-stone, hard and unkind, only something disciplined and enduring.

I walked round the graveyard, searching for her name, trying at the same time to find some kind of historical pattern in the growth of the graveyard in order to narrow my search. But shiny new gravestones were mingled with worn ones. There was no order that I could discern. Perhaps people had been buried in spots chosen at random, or clustered according to family and kinship.

After an hour of painstaking work, I knew that I couldn't determine whether Jolene Galant lay under that thinly-covered soil. A number of the gravestones were illegible. In some cases this was due to age and weathering; others couldn't be read because the names and dates had been scratched on prefabricated material with a nail, and so hadn't lasted long. There were many unmarked graves, only weathered mounds remaining. Sadly, a great many of these were small, and there were many small graves too that were marked: poverty had taken its toll of the children.

I left the burial ground and approached a middle-aged man watching me from his gate, his face a picture of indifferent curiosity. I asked him if there was an old-aged home in the village.

'No, Miss,' he replied. 'Pniel is a family town. We don't do that. We look after our own.'

'They don't go to an old-aged home then?'

'No, unless they want to. Only then.'

'So there are some old people who end up in old-aged homes? It's not totally unknown?'

'No, it's not unknown.'

'Where do they go then?'

'There's one in Paarl. They go there.'

He couldn't tell me the name of the old-aged home in

Paarl, a much larger town not far away. I thanked him and slowly walked back to the church, digesting my impressions: the trees, the water, the graveyard, the church.

I asked a passerby where the dominee lived. He pointed out the manse, which was behind the fountain in the piazza. Perhaps the dominee could give me more information about the old-aged homes; perhaps he might know Jolene Galant, or what had become of her.

My spirits lifted at the sight of the open windows of the manse; he was sure to be there. But there was no one home. I looked about. There were a few girls about my own age chatting beside a cypress tree. Could they tell me, I asked, the dominee's name? One of them told me: Daniels. Did they know his phone number perhaps? No, they didn't. I thanked them and walked back to my car.

I sat in that warm interior, summarising what I had learnt. It filled much less than a shorthand notebook page. So hard, I reflected, to collect information directly. I was used to the power of books, of libraries, so much information held together, far more than any one person could use. Now I had to tramp through graveyards and ask questions, and search for people who might or might not know the answers. I decided to return to Cape Town, and contact the absent dominee and find the old-aged home by phone.

A week went by, and I let Jolene slide. I did get round to phoning Koen, and made an appointment to see him in Franschhoek on the weekend. This time I said nothing about a history project — I presented it as a social call. I drove out, planning strategies to turn our conversation into an interview as unobtrusively as possible. I had a little tape recorder in my cloth bag. I planned to turn it on sneakily and get him reminiscing about old times. It was nonsense, of course. He would inevitably notice which way the conversation was going.

When I got there, a servant I had never met answered the door.

'I've come to see Mr Sieberhagen,' I said. 'Can I come in?'

She stood in the doorway and replied, 'Mr Sieberhagen is sleeping, Madam.'

'At this time of the morning?'

'He's not feeling well, Madam.'

'But he knew I was coming! He could have let me know!'

She just smiled at me and waited.

I shook my head in frustration and said, 'And please don't call me Madam.'

She opened her mouth and closed it and waited.

'Please tell him Jessica came,' I said, and left. I stopped in at a coffee shop on the way out, and sat there thinking. I was sure Koen was stringing me along. This was my second attempt to interview him for my history project. The first time he had fallen asleep. Now he was — so conveniently — sick. I couldn't begin to imagine why, but I was increasingly suspicious that there might be good reason for his evasiveness.

The street map was wrong about Bauhinia Street in Paarl where Vredehof is located, an old-aged home serving the coloured community. But I found it eventually, by questioning pedestrian after pedestrian, each of whom sent me roughly in the right direction.

It was a relatively modern complex of single story buildings, easily recognised: scores of old people sat in the sun, talking, listening to the radio, or just drinking up sunlight and their memories. It was surrounded by an eight foot high fence. A security guard manned the wire gate. I wondered why they needed that kind of protection, and assumed that there might be gangster activity in the community. Across the road from Vredehof were three storey apartment blocks, sub-economic units, paint peeling off the window frames and washing on every conceivable framework — fire escapes, railings, lines across balconies — and children and underfed animals everywhere.

The guard took me inside, where I explained myself and was taken to the marketing manager. I explained my mission again and he took me to the general manager, Mrs Carelse, a short, wide, unruffled woman. I explained myself once more, and she said, 'No, my dear, we don't have a Mrs Galant here. We have sixty-three single women, and five more married couples, and the men. But there's no Mrs Galant, I can tell you that without checking the records.'

I must have been visibly disappointed, because she offered to show me round. I accepted out of politeness rather than any real interest. I retain impressions of dingy yellow-ochre walls, low ceilings, dark passages. There was a large, well-lit lounge, with many arched steel windows, and nearly fifty old people sitting in the chairs, some watching television, their bodies stooped and wrinkled, their clothing dull, their movements timid, stunned by the passage of time. And then there was a sewing room, a warm close barrel of toothless herrings who looked up at me in kind amusement and greeted me warmly and went back to their sewing. But I was more preoccupied with the fact that there was no Mrs Galant, and hardly listened to Mrs Carelse's commentary. Then the obvious occurred to me at last: 'You have records, don't you, Mrs Carelse?' I asked.

'Yes, of course,' she replied placidly.

'On computer, or on paper?'

'No, we have ordinary files. Paper.'

'You wouldn't have the women's maiden names in these files?'

She nodded: 'Oh yes. And some of them are spinsters, you see.'

'What if the person I'm looking for was married? Would you have her maiden name on record?'

'We would, yes. But then we would have to look through *all* the files because we don't know her married name. And then, my dear, what if she was here under her married name and then died?'

'What do you do with the deceased? The files, I mean.'

'We keep them in our safe, in case of family inquiries.'

I wondered how far I could go, then took the plunge: 'Do you think I would be allowed to look through those files?'

'No, I don't think we could allow that.'

She didn't seem particularly displeased by my request, so I asked, 'Would you mind terribly if I asked you to look through the files for Galant as a maiden name? At least through the files of the, ah, those still alive?'

To my surprise and relief she nodded and said, 'Yes, that's alright. I don't mind doing it. But not now. I'm too busy just now.'

I thanked her profusely, and left my phone number with her. As I threaded my way out of the neglected township, my excitement at making some progress died away. I didn't think she would do anything about it.

Various other dead-ends followed. I tried the Pensions Office of the relevant government department, and was so impressed by the spectacle of administrative chaos I encountered that I decided to look elsewhere. I phoned Dominee Daniels of the Dutch Reformed Church at Pniel. He didn't know anyone by that name, or any Jolene at all except three little girls; but he was new to the area and promised to make enquiries. I spent two days at the South African Library, hoping to find a notice on the death of Jolene Galant, or perhaps an advertisement for her services. There was no Franschhoek newspaper in the reference section, but there was the *Paarl Post* on microfilm. I scanned the personal and employment columns of every issue on record since 1937, but of course there was no mention of Jolene Galant.

I had almost decided to give up on the history project as I had planned it — to change the topic, hand in something flimsy and hope to squeak through. Then my great-uncle Koen phoned me.

'Jessica,' he said, 'I want you to come and see me.'

My eyes widened. I said, 'I'm dying to see you, Oom Koen. What about this afternoon?'

'No, that's too soon. I'm not feeling well.'

'I'm sorry to hear that —'

'No, it's nothing, just a chest cold. I'm half over it.'

I arranged to see him on Sunday, and that is where the conversation ended. I felt a vague pessimism. I feared that he would cancel the arrangement at the last minute again.

10

I went on my own to see a suite of contemporary South African ballets. I stood in the crowded lobby during the first interval with a glass of champagne in my hand, musing over the performance. My blood ran cold suddenly, and then I realised why: a familiar portly figure was approaching.

'Good evening, Ms Kruger,' said Teboso Ngqayimbana, his voice particularly sibilant.

I've had your cock in my mouth, I thought, and you call me Ms Kruger. I blushed at my own thought, but for once didn't mind blushing. I have a floral nature, I realised, as the image of a scarlet hibiscus rose in my mind. Beneath it, stout green leaves.

'Teboso, how nice to see you,' I said, as bitchily as possible.

'Have you enjoyed the performance so far?' he asked.

'An interesting fusion of African and Western forms ...'

'I myself thought it was so much grunting, and wriggling, and anal writhing.'

'I take that as a comment,' I said coldly, 'on my own taste rather than the choreographer's.'

He uttered a brief cash register laugh: 'Ms Kruger at her best.'

The conversation might have ended there — I drank my champagne and gazed at the oddly assorted crowd and waited for him to go away — then he placed his hand on my forearm. My skin reacted to his touch with an odd electric discharge, an audible snap of static. He jerked his hand away.

'You are not only a poltergeist, Ms Kruger, you are a human torpedo ray.'

'What are you talking about, Mr Ngqayimbana?'

'You are a danger to this theatre. What if you ignite, you know, burst into spontaneous combustion?'

Soft gongs insisted we return to our seats.

'If I do that,' I retorted, 'You can throw your champagne over me.'

The appearance of a downright sexual greed in his face startled me.

'You'd like that, wouldn't you, Mr Ngqayimbana?' I asked. He looked at me oddly.

The gongs rang again. I drained my champagne, rested my hand briefly on his — warm to the touch, no static snap this time — and said, 'Goodbye, Teboso.'

He just nodded. I left him and returned to my seat.

My inner reaction to that encounter was a more demanding performance than the one on stage. My skin crawled, my soul filled with wilder contortions than any contemporary South African dance. After twenty minutes of this I let out a shuddering sigh, then glanced round furtively to see if anyone had noticed. I slumped back in my seat and concentrated on the ballet. Ngqayimbana, I thought, you great black worm.

He was there at the second interval. We rubbed shoulders at the bar. 'Ah, Ms Kruger!' he exclaimed, as if surprised to see me.

We threaded our way out of the crush and turned to face each other.

'You're edgy tonight, Mr Ngqayimbana. You're making me edgy. I don't like it.'

'I am sorry, Ms Kruger,' he said gravely. 'That was not my intention.'

We sipped champagne as an awkward silence grew more awkward. I didn't want to leave him yet, but I didn't know how or where to move. There are times when the skin of events peels away for me, and interaction become blindingly clear, as if soul touches directly on soul. But so often things are fudged by the thumbprints of conversation, by the nonsense we talk, by the rules of evasion that force us to talk it. Weariness filled me. I longed to speak the simple truth that lay between us.

I was suddenly able to do so: 'There's a reason for all this, Teboso — for this tension.'

'Why are we so uncomfortable with each other, Ms Kruger?'

No such moment of truth had afflicted Teboso; he remained cynical and defensive. I felt it, but wasn't deterred.

'Jessica,' I replied gently. 'Call me Jessica.'

A strange mood had taken me. I felt calm, despite the adrenalin coursing through my blood, despite my racing heart.

'I can't speak for you, Teboso, but the explanation is simple. I want to fuck you. I need to.'

His expression was a sudden riot of alarm.

'I think you want the same thing,' I added. 'Well, I'll be surprised if you don't.'

Still no response from Ngqayimbana.

'And,' I completed the explanation, 'we're not letting it happen.'

Still struggling to compose himself, very earnestly, he said, 'Yes, Jessica, I do. Yes, we're not.'

Then he stuck out his hand and I shook it as if we had reached a gentlemen's agreement.

The evening continued at its own bizarre pace. We returned to our separate seats. I felt lame with excitement and dread. I couldn't focus on the dancing at all. My mind went blank and the ballet became a sequence of meaningless movement, a kinetic language I couldn't decipher. The applause was endless, and I wished the dancers would leave their elegant bowing and scraping, and disappear.

We found each other in the lobby afterwards. 'Will you come home with me tonight, Jessica?' he asked, resting his hand on my shoulder. 'Will you? Do you really want to?'

'Yes,' I replied, 'I suppose I do.'

He brought me to him, and for the first time since I had known him we kissed, formally, chastely.

We sat down on his bed, facing that indecently big mirror, almost the size of the wall itself. The pair of us stared back, a pair of mismatched chessmen.

He leaned over and carefully unlaced his shoes. 'I once dreamt,' he remarked absently, 'that three kinds of magic are necessary. By magic, of course, the dream signified types of knowledge, as much as three kinds of power.'

He stood up and removed his trousers, folding them neatly. I followed his cue and began undressing.

'The first kind of knowledge was called scalar magic. The second was named trefoil in the dream, and the third was the, ah, asynchronous.'

As I took off my bra, he put his spectacles back on. To see my breasts in the mirror, I supposed.

He focused on them and said, 'Now I know that scalar magic was just, you know, scientific discourse, rational thinking.'

I removed my skirt.

'And trefoil magic is theosophical or arcane wisdom, I should say, the language of the Mysteries. Today it is mostly found buried in literature or art, in cryptic form.'

By now only my tights were left. He stood there without trousers, a bespectacled talking machine with a great big erection sticking out from under his shirt: 'The asynchronous magic is different, something that of itself —'

'Teboso,' I said, 'For God's sake, shut up.'

I pushed him down on the bed and climbed on top of

him. I will not set down in any detail what happened next. Just a few impressions. Glancing at him fully naked, in the mirror, I saw that my lover was a bear, a chocolate bear with tight black coils of hair all over; a plump bear wrapped around a thin Caucasian female with large breasts and visible ribs, skin reddening everywhere with pleasure and embarrassment. I would like to add that the entry of his penis hurt, and I'm not sure that the subsequent delight — at least this first time — was worth the pain. Let me state for the record that he wore a condom. He didn't want to, but I insisted; my mother would have been proud of me.

In the end, despite all reservations, it was a great success. I came, in a crescendo of ecstatic shrieks. On the last high note, Teboso's great wall mirror cracked and cracked again, the flaw running diagonally across the whole frame with a sound not unlike grinding teeth.

'That is what I wanted to say,' he muttered breathlessly. He groped for his spectacles, couldn't find them, and stared at the ruptured mirror. 'Asynchronous magic. Psychic energy.' He gestured at the crack. 'It comes out of nowhere, it disrupts order and destroys sequence. It defies analysis, it irrupts. Breaks, you know, into the given.'

'That's all crap, Teboso,' I said. 'I'm just a little old poltergeist. Leave it at that.'

He left it at that. I lay with my head on his chest, listening to the beat of his heart, which was more interesting to me than his conversation.

I should add that we lived happily ever after.

One breakthrough after another. I needn't have worried about Koen's capriciousness. I was admitted, my uncle looked quite well, and he even had coffee and biscuits waiting for me.

When we had settled down, he said, 'You wanted me to tell you something about your grandparents.'

'Yes, I did. I particularly wanted to know about —'

'And the maid, you said.'

I nodded.

I reached out for the tape recorder. My hand stopped in mid-air and I found myself staring at him. What might Koen think of this procedure, I wondered suddenly. What would he think of all this — the term 'silly-buggery' came to mind, a phrase he might have used — this vapid human-istic resuscitation of the past, so long dead, irremediably dead?

'And so?' he asked. 'Are you going to stay like that all morning?'

I found no way to explain my reaction to him. I avoid-ed the question. 'Do you mind if I tape what you say?' I asked instead.

'No, I don't mind. But listen now, Jessica. What exactly do you want me to say? I'm still not really sure what you have in mind.'

'I have to write a short history of my family, covering a certain period. It has to be an oral history. That means I must interview people who lived through that time — I need living sources of information. I can't say beforehand what you must tell me.'

'No, Jessica, I'm still a bit confused here.'

I closed my eyes and collected myself. I said, 'Look, let's keep it simple. Tell me the story, that's all. Anyone can tell a story — tell me what you know, just as it comes.'

You can be Oom Schalk Lourens, I thought.

'Well then,' he replied, a bit doubtfully. But he took a few sips of coffee and began to relate his tale. 'I can't remember exactly when it was. It would have been before the war years in any event, in the late thirties. Your grand-father was newly married to my sister, and they came to Franschhoek, where they settled down in a rented house. Eugene was lecturing at the training college there. He taught them science. He was a bright man, Eugene. I can see you have his brains.'

I nodded, agreeing at least with the latter.

'Well, it was going very nicely, and he was teaching away,

but then things started to go wrong. He started indoctrinating his students with the theory of evolution. You know, Darwin and so on.'

'And that created a problem?' I asked, smiling at the thought.

'It sounds stupid now. You can say anything you like these days, no-one really cares what you say. But things were different then, Jessica, very different. People worried about this evolution matter because we all knew it came out of liberalism, you see. And because it denied the Bible story of Creation. Things like that were very important. When I was your age, people took the Bible as it was, as it was written. There was a tremendous hoo-ha, and he got into trouble. He nearly lost his job, I believe. In the end they just warned him very firmly to stop his nonsense.'

'And did he?'

'Of course. He had no choice.'

Koen stopped there. We both stared at the tape recorder. It hissed quietly away.

'Is there anything else you can tell me about this incident?' I prompted.

'I don't think so. I don't know that much about it. I wasn't much involved. Anfra, now, she was very upset by the whole business. She was very religious — still is, of course — she found it very upsetting, very difficult.'

'What sort of person was Eugene? What was he like?'

Koen stared pensively out the window. 'I must tell you that I didn't really like him. We never took to each other. And there was the whole scandal with the maid, you know, and what it did to my sister. It soured our relationship because, being an interfering young upstart, I did get mixed up in the fiasco. But to answer your question: your grandfather had us all fooled. We all thought he was a steady man. Dry, boring perhaps, but reliable.'

The old man laughed gently, and wiped his hand across his mouth. 'Eugene was quite a devil, really.'

'I have diabolic genes then,' I said, 'ignoring my grandmother's saintly contribution.'

Koen ignored the comment.

'And what was the scandal exactly?' I asked.

'The scandal?' He looked at me importantly and said, 'I can tell you something, Jessica: this was probably the greatest scandal that has ever hit the town of Franschhoek.'

'Do tell, Oom Koen.'

'Or it would have been if I hadn't done something about it. Oh yes, I couldn't let it go on. Your grandfather was making a fool of himself with a coloured woman. I warned him to stop. I warned him a number of times. But do you think he would listen to me?'

And so I heard at last the improbable tale of Anfra and Eugene Kruger, of Eugene's love for Jolene Galant, and what my great-uncle Koen Sieberhagen did to bring matters to a head. When his account had come to an end, I thought for a moment, tapped my pencil on my teeth, and said: 'Just to clarify something ... You say you offered her a job on one of your farms, to get her away from the Krugers. So she worked there for a while. After that, what happened to her? Where did she go?'

'God knows. She just left. No goodbye, no thank you, nothing. As shiftless as all her people. In fact, I was stupid to expect any gratitude. For all I know, she might even be dead.' He grinned: 'She's old enough to be dead, just like me.' As the grin faded he asked, 'Have you tried looking in the graveyard at Pniel? I don't say she's there of course, but you could try your luck. The people there are very loyal to their little town. Maybe she came home in the end.'

Eugene

Near Steynsrus/Franschhoek, 1937

1

Let all things begin with holy matrimony. So said the minister in his small bleak church. What God has put together let no man sunder. A man goes out from his family unto his wife and they are one flesh. How goodly are thy tents, O Jacob, thy herds, thy flocks.

All through the ceremony that bound him in marriage to Anfra Sieberhagen, Eugene Kruger frowned. He wasn't sure that he wanted to be married in a church. He had no objection to religious ceremonies in general, but he was bothered by an obscure feeling he couldn't quite identify. As he went through the motions, his thoughts circled back to this resentment, this dissonance. What was it? Whenever he was about to grasp it, he was asked to do something or say something, and the thought escaped him. He rebuked himself, and gave his wonderful bride and his marriage to her the attention they deserved.

Anfra wasn't frowning. She was suitably rapt. She was beautiful in her white gown, her veil, her train of silk imported at great cost from Lourenço Marques, fetched by dog-cart from the station at Steynsrus. But she was deeply worried almost to the point of feeling sick about being made one flesh. Hers was pure, sweet and untested by any caustic male impression: a great change was to come on her.

It distressed her too that her normally good natured and reasonable bridegroom was frowning. Her more malicious relatives (she admitted the hurt only in her innermost thoughts) might see it as a slap in the face.

She concentrated, licked once at the corner of her mouth, and soon was the wife — possessed at last, sealed with a golden ring — of Eugene Kruger.

In Koen Sieberhagen's book, Eugene was a dry stick. True, he was an excellent shot: why, just a few days before he had sent a leaping springbok spinning, taken neatly through the head at two hundred paces. But his hands were always clean, he was often seen reading, and he wouldn't submit to the stag party Koen wanted to hold for him. 'It's a bloody insult,' Koen complained to his father privately. Old Barend Sieberhagen just shook his head. Although Koen didn't know what his father meant, he was used to such cryptic gestures. He decided that his father agreed it was an insult, but that he should ignore it for the sake of his sister's future happiness.

At the reception, Koen made a speech in which he welcomed his new brother-in-law to the family, praising his scholarly qualities — 'We've never had a thinking man among us, or a man as highly educated as a college lecturer, so from now on we'll have to watch out what we say.' It sounded as if he meant that the family would have to start thinking about the things they said instead of just saying them. This was funny because it was obviously an alien practice; but everyone understood him to mean he would have to stop swearing as much as he did, which was even funnier.

Then Koen pointed out that he had been instrumental in getting Eugene his new job in Franschhoek where, as a farmer in his own right, undertaker and local Chevrolet dealer, he had more than a little influence. Eugene just smiled. Finally, Koen raised his glass of witblits, fifty-five per cent impure alcohol innocent of ageing or contact with wood, and toasted the happy couple. Everyone stood up and sang 'How the hell can we believe him?' and the dancing began in earnest.

The lamp in the guest bedroom cast a gentle oily smell. Insect sounds, gentler sounds of leaf and wind, came through the rough stone walls. And Eugene thought: How goodly are thy tents, O Jacob.

The door opened and out of the dark passage came his wife, tented in her cotton smock. Her dark hair was braided, her eyes were frightened. These were strong eyes, not comfortable with fear; her lips were pressed tightly together.

'Here,' he said, patting the bed beside him. 'Come sit with me.' Anfra sat down beside him and the mattress sagged, rolling them together.

'Eugene,' she said. 'My darling.' She smiled. 'My husband now.' He bent towards her to kiss her; she responded chastely. He took her face in his large hard hands and pressed her towards him, kissing more urgently. She pulled back: 'Eugene,' she said, 'Eugene.' Her scent clouded his mind and he couldn't think. A sharp intake of breath from her, and she protested again.

'Yes, my love. What is it?'

'Aren't we going to read from the Bible? Before we go to sleep?'

Eugene closed his eyes and opened them. 'Yes dear. Of course.'

She pointed. 'It's there, in the dresser.'

He looked at the dresser and back at her. Yes, she meant it.

She said, 'Aren't you going to get the Bible? We can't just go to sleep like the heathen do.'

He slid out of bed and fetched the book.

'What are we going to read, my love?' she asked. 'You must select something.'

He opened it hastily and began reading: 'In the beginning, God created the heaven and the earth ... '

Anfra studied his profile as he read, lit by warm lamplight. She felt terribly safe with him, and cherished, and she thought: What a wonderful, noble, fine man my husband is. But she realised — it was a shadow fallen across her light — that his terrible frown was back.

He put the Bible down then and turned to her, taking her in his arms. 'Eugene,' she said. 'Eugene, please.'

He leaned back on his pillows and looked at her. Nothing could extinguish the natural kindness of his gaze. 'What is it, Anfra?'

'The lamp,' she said. 'Put it out.' She had often enough observed cows and horses and sheep and pigs and chickens and ducks mating, and didn't want to be seen in that light.

As it happened, once her gown was lifted she grew very tense, even though it was dark and nothing could be seen at all, so tense that the marriage wasn't consummated on the first night.

Eugene sat opposite Anfra, reading. The train wheels thundered as they passed through a tunnel and the sweet stink of coalsmoke poured suddenly into their compartment. Eugene closed the window. Anfra sat with her hands on her lap, very upright. Her eyes looked strained; she had a headache. She held a handkerchief which she knotted around her middle finger and released and knotted again. He looked up at her, smiled abstractedly, and returned to his book.

'Eugene,' she said at last and waited for his attention. 'Eugene.' When he looked up he saw that her lips were firmly compressed; now her fingers were still. 'This is difficult for me,' she said. She went pale, then she flushed, and blurted out: 'I didn't want to talk about it, but I have given it thought, and we are man and wife, and so we must be honest with each other about our feelings.'

Eugene closed his book patiently.

'I feel guilty asking you this question, because it is a very small thing.'

She stopped, and to encourage her he asked, 'What is this question?'

'When we were married — during our marriage I saw you frowning your way through the dominee's address. It looked as if you were angry and my heart sank.'

'But my darling —'

She put her hand up: 'No, Eugene, let me finish now,

otherwise I will never be able to say another word about this. Then I notice that half the time we're together you still have this look on your face.' She peered at him in terrible anxious appeal. 'You were never like that when we were courting. Have I done anything? Are you unhappy with me?'

He raised his hands and dropped them helplessly. 'I am amazed. I am amazed. My poor dear. I had no idea that — frowning, you say?'

She nodded, unhappily.

He passed his hand over his brow.

'It is true that I have been perplexed about a certain question. Perhaps that is why you see me frowning.'

'And what is this question? Is it something I may ask about?'

'Of course it is, Anfra. There is nothing secret about this question, nothing of a confidential or intimate nature, if that is what you mean.'

She didn't answer, but gazed at him intently as if all her happiness to come depended on his next words. He paused as he gathered his thoughts and finally replied, 'It is a question of the Bible, and the dominee's words. The same question comes up in the passage I read on our wedding night in the... in the bedroom.'

She gestured, unable to frame any words to reflect her apprehension.

'Have you read anything about the theory of evolution?'

'Well, no, but of course I know the idea — that man is descended from the apes —'

He leaned forward, and his enthusiasm glowed as he spoke: 'It is more complicated than that, much more complicated. Few natural scientists today question this view. But there is much disagreement, you see, about the manner in which inherited qualities change over the generations.'

'But what has that to do with the dominee? Or our wedding? And why should it make you angry?'

'No no, I'm not angry. It doesn't make me angry. It is

just a question for which I have no answer. At least, the answers I have are insufficient.'

'But I still don't understand: what exactly is the question?'

'How can you talk of the divine creation of man when there is such weighty evidence for the mutation and development of species through natural processes?'

'But the dominee said nothing about that!'

'Exactly!' he said triumphantly.

Anfra patted her brow with her twisted handkerchief. The khaki soil and stone of the Karoo passed endlessly outside the window, posing and answering no questions. 'I have a very strange new husband,' she said. But her relief was palpable.

Eugene leant back against the green leather seat and closed his eyes. The pleasing rhythms of the train traveled through his frame, leading him back into the pathways of speculation. Could changes acquired or learnt in one single generation be transmitted to the next? Was it true, as Lamarck believed, that the children of weight-lifters would also have strong arm and shoulder muscles? He gave thought to his brother-in-law, Koen, who was as garrulous as his father was taciturn.

He realised he was frowning again, and smoothed his face over. The frown sprang back before long.

That night in the coupé Eugene and Anfra Kruger tried to make love for the second time. Even though the frown had been explained (if not exactly removed), love was not yet possible. Eugene resolved once again to be extremely patient with his bride.

It is a staggering view: the zinc-roofed street curves downhill, and at the end of it the town stops, just disappears from sight. Hillside vineyards take over, climbing the mountain wall south of Franschhoek in russet steps. They had just come to their newly rented house, which was large and ramshackle and placed on an even more neglected plot. We shall be the kings of nothing, thought Eugene, feasting on what we see.

Anfra bit her lip. 'This house,' she said. 'It needs so much work.'

'There,' he said, pointing to a stream running under the fence, thinly sedged: 'We can have ducks.' He gestured widely: 'Plenty of room for a garden, and we can keep hens as well. Bantams. Keep the snails down.'

'You can have poultry or flowers,' she said. 'Not both. They scratch up the seeds.'

He smiled: 'Fruit trees too: plum and apple, and avocado. We shall feast on fruit all year round and on duck eggs in winter!'

She smoothed down her skirt. 'That's not a fruiting plum, Eugene. And that isn't an apple tree either. I think it's a quince.'

He pointed at a shrub with rust on the leaves: 'I believe that is a cumquat! How marvellous!'

'They're completely inedible unless you make marmalade. And duck eggs smell.'

'Not if they're very fresh.' At last her dismay penetrated: 'We don't really have to have ducks,' he added soothingly. 'It's just an idea. Or make marmalade.'

An image of cumquats stung with blue mould rose in his mind: slowly decomposing sacs sagging in the grass, little ruined planets.

'It's so big,' she said. 'The house is so big. Why?'

'For all our children,' he said teasingly. 'A child in each room. Two children, three per room, we shall lose count.'

She actually paled. 'Come,' he said, extending his hand to her, not noticing.

'The real reason,' he said as the gate creaked open, 'is that it was cheap. I could afford the rent, and it comes furnished. Well, some of the rooms are furnished. At least, there is some furniture.'

He opened the front door and smiled at her: 'Welcome home.' But Anfra didn't smile back. Her eyes closed instead and her knees sagged and she fell slowly onto them, collapsing forward until her forehead rested on the ground. Then she keeled over onto her side.

He leant beside her in alarm. There was no colour in her face; her breathing was even and shallow. Before he could think what to do, her eyelids shook and opened, and she stared at him in confusion. They closed again and she sank back. Eugene Kruger lifted his unconscious bride and carried her over the threshold.

He lowered her onto the first mattress he could find. It was naked and dust rose as it settled under her weight, making him sneeze. She probably needs iron, he thought.

When Doctor van Aswegen came later in the day, he confirmed this diagnosis and recommended plenty of liver. The problem was that Anfra was a delicate eater, not fond of meat, offal least of all.

Dusk. She lay on her bed, now beaten and made up, her eyes darkly reflective. The mattress sagged in the middle and when she turned over the springs creaked and groaned. I am like the bed, she thought, a decrepit thing. Eugene brought her a bowl of soup the doctor's wife had sent over. She said, 'I'm sorry. I feel so stupid. I'm sorry I was such a cow.'

'How could you help it? It's the iron. Doctor van Aswegen said so.'

'It's easy to say it's the iron,' she said. 'Why didn't I faint yesterday then?'

'It is the iron. I looked under your eyelids myself, I also thought they were whitish.'

The thought pulsed wanly under her skin, in her blood: when you said many children I couldn't breathe, I was hurled down. And there was a picture which she couldn't see, but was there, a presence in her imagination: a large round doll's head, something she must love, yet tearing her apart.

'Of course all organisms have to adapt,' Eugene said. 'Everything is new for you here. This is a new world. You have a new husband and a new life. I can understand the difficulty.'

She smiled wanly: 'Men understand everything.'

'Quite so,' he responded.

She rested her hand on his much larger one, drawing strength from its ample and patient warmth.

After Anfra had gone to sleep he sat on the stoep, staring into the moonless night. By nine-thirty it appeared that the whole street had gone to bed too; not a single window in the street showed any light.

The breeze made dry oak and plane leaves scutter down the paving, and harder bluegum leaves rattle on their branches like swords. He lit one of his small cheroots, his first of the day, and sucked appreciatively. Survival of the fittest, he thought vaguely (the thought a loose leaf, unconnected to any tree) must imply a suppression of the unfit, death for those variations which cannot adapt. Could this be applied to the life of a human soul? The cloud he blew out was snatched away. Long after his cheroot had burnt out he sat resting on the bench until a feeling of pleasant wooden belonging overcame him. Like the furniture, like the old house with its many rooms, this town was his place in the great world, even if his wife had fainted entering.

It is eternally hot in Franschhoek. Johann Schuitema, third year student at the Teacher Training College there, tugged at his tie and put his hand up. Eugene paused and arched an eyebrow. 'Mr Schuitema?'

'Sir,' said Mr Schuitema, and stopped. Body heat filtered through serge suits, radiating into the small, already sweltering classroom. He mopped his brow. It was difficult to think.

There was a knock on the door. Eugene opened it. The factotum, old Mentoor, stood in the corridor with a slip of paper on a clip-board. He thrust it wordlessly at Eugene who read it and said, 'A notice from the rector. You may remove your jackets, gentlemen.'

A general sigh of relief. Waves of heat rose almost visibly as the jackets came off. Eugene removed his as well.

Johann Schuitema was still standing. 'Your question, Mr Schuitema. We're still waiting for it.'

'Mr Kruger, you say about this theory of evolution that … if I understand … higher organisms develop gradually from the lower.'

'Yes, that is correct.'

'So, then man is just a different kind of animal: basically the same as an ape, but more complex.'

'Well, that is one of the implications of Darwin's theory. It is of course, a theory — it remains to be proven in all its central aspects. One problem is to demonstrate the missing link in the chain of evolution from ape to man. About twenty years ago, a chap by the name of Charles Dawson found a large, round, shall we say "modern" skull, one capable of housing a sophisticated brain. The find was on a Pleistocene site in England, together with some implements of bone and flint that had been quite clearly worked — they weren't just picked up and put to use, you see. The important thing about this specimen is that the jawbone was typical of what you'd find on a large ape.'

'Typical of what you'd find on an Englishman,' interjected Hendrik Gouws, the class wag.

Eugene laughed. 'Be careful, Mr Gouws. My great-grandfather was an Englishman.'

General laughter at the sally.

'A find,' resumed Eugene, 'that generated considerable excitement, as you can well understand. Now this man — named Piltdown Man in honour of the site at which he was unearthed — might well be the missing link, having important characteristics of both ape and man, rather than that splendid fellow Pithecanthropus.

'Now more recently, there has been some doubt expressed as to exactly how old the site is. In any event, the debate continues. Science does not deal in unshakable certainties, though it is precisely this point that many scientists miss.

'Still, to answer your question, Mr Schuitema, if Darwin is correct, man is most probably descended from ape-like ancestors.'

'I see, Sir.' He sat down, looking troubled.

'Now to continue with the actual mechanism of species transmission ...' Eugene continued. He turned round and began sketching rapidly on the board.

He turned back. Nicolas Jacobus Gerhardus Severus Kriegler had raised his hand. He was thin, with a schooled ascetic face; he was also the only student still wearing his jacket, and limp strands of brown hair clung to his temple. 'Mr Kruger,' he said, 'May I ask you a question?'

'By all means, Mr Kriegler. What is the question?'

'With the greatest respect to yourself, Mr Kruger, I have difficulty with what you are saying.'

'And what is your difficulty, Mr Kriegler?'

The student picked up a black leather-bound book and brandished it. 'This book tells me several things which I am inclined to believe. One of these things is that our Heavenly Father is responsible for the creation of man. Another thing that I believe is that man was created by the Almighty in His own image. A third is that the Lord God has given man stewardship over His creation, over the beasts in the field and the birds in the air.

'To my humble understanding, this means that man is set over and against the kingdom of the animals. He is not a part of that kingdom. He is not of the same substance, he is not of the same kind. Man is a spiritual being, and not a bestial creature, in the same category as the beasts in the field and so on.'

There were murmurs of assent in the class.

'Now it appears, Sir, that your teaching would imply otherwise. Pardon me for raising this objection, but I cannot do otherwise and yet profess my Christian faith with any integrity.'

The book came to rest quietly on the desk and Nicolas Kriegler sat down.

Eugene looked round the class. It seemed that there were many who shared this point of view. 'Please, Mr Kriegler,' he replied, 'you must never apologise for raising your questions. But I wonder if you are training for the right profession?'

Nicolas Jacobus Gerhardus Severus Kriegler blinked.

'I was only joking, Mr Kriegler. About the profession.'

No response.

Eugene cleared his throat. 'However, this is not the first time your objection has been brought up. I think we can take your question one step further. If random selection is the mechanism behind evolution, how can there be a creator God?'

A frisson ran through the group, raw dissonance felt under the skin; but Kriegler nodded.

'I have given it a great deal of thought,' said Eugene, 'and I cannot say that I have the wisdom necessary to resolve this dilemma. On the one hand, we have the apparent certainty of science. On the other, the certainty of revelation, of scripture. We cannot ignore the claims of either, yet they contradict each other. The only answer I can give is that there is faith and scripture on the one hand, and reason and scientific method on the other. Different forms of understanding that serve different purposes. My belief is that they describe different things.'

There was now a mood of perplexity in the class. Perhaps, thought Eugene later, a mood of ugly perplexity. There was no time to discuss it further, because Mentoor was going down the corridor and up the stairs ringing the bell for tea.

At teatime, Eugene sat next to Oom Deon Viljoen. Oom Deon was the old English master, a teacher now past retirement who still taught there because no suitable replacement had been found for several years running. He was a thin tall gentleman with refined features, who always wore white linen suits, and who raised his finger and spoke with a satisfied, joyful pedantry. Eugene sat next to Oom Deon because his predecessor had sat next to Oom Deon, and lecturers at Franschhoek Teacher Training College always sat in the same chairs when they drank tea or held meetings.

'It is a strange paradox to me,' said Oom Deon, 'that although tea is a very hot drink, it cools one down. Now this paradox is the greatest contribution of the British Empire to the hotter countries south of the equator.' He pronounced equator with great clarity and satisfaction, and sipped his steaming tea thus cooling himself.

'If I may ask, Eugene,' he continued, 'how is it with the marriage?'

Eugene nodded gravely. 'Fine, thank you, Oom Deon. Things are going very well.'

'That is good,' said Oom Deon. 'I must tell you that I have great sympathy for the newlywed. I remember that my first year of marriage was an absolute nightmare. I didn't know what I was doing.' His gaze turned inwards and he laughed gently: 'I didn't have a clue!'

Eugene ducked behind his teacup: 'No, things are fine.'

'Of course, you must realise that you have to adapt to each other, as well as to a whole new situation. You are in a new town, a new job, and a completely new life-situation.' The finger went up. 'That is the thing.'

Eugene sipped. It was true; the tea did have a cooling effect, more as an after-effect.

'I remember that when we were first married, my wife and I fought like cat and dog. We were terribly in love, but didn't understand each other's ways. We had to learn, you see. We had to learn from each other.'

'Actually, Oom Deon, we're getting on nicely, thank you.'

Oom Deon touched Eugene's knee and leaned closer. 'Eugene, there is one thing you must not worry about. In this strange modern society of ours they make a great fuss about it, but I have learnt that it is not so terribly important.'

'And what is that, Oom Deon?'

The English master leaned even closer and whispered, the syllables rolling out separated, distinct: 'You must not worry about simultaneous orgasm! I believe it is not even strictly speaking necessary.'

'Thank you for that advice, Oom Deon.' Eugene placed his teacup firmly on the saucer.

Anfra opened her shutters and stepped out of the bedroom. The cement floor of the stoep was cool and dusty and soothed her feet. It was past midnight, the air was warm, an unkind heat that cheated the body of rest. But what breeze there was cooled the moisture in the folded secrets of her body, made it easier to breathe, relieved the pressure of her temples. She didn't hear the stream that trickled under the fence or the chorus of its frogs, or the trilling of crickets, because she was asleep: Anfra was sleepwalking, a dark-haired figure in a white cotton gown drifting along the stoep.

With a delicate crunch, she destroyed a snail in her path. The impression of its cold remnants boiling up between her toes halted her progress. She turned slightly, hand outstretched. Then she stepped off the stoep, accurately, the wet grass folding over her feet and ankles, and walked into the garden.

The splintering of the snailshell carried an impossible distance, waking Eugene. He had taken to sleeping alone on the creaking sofa; now he opened his eyes wondering what had woken him and what part of his life this was. He threw off the single sheet and went to his wife's bedroom. She wasn't there, but the curtains shifting limply beside the open shutters told him where to look. He stepped out and saw her, followed her off the stoep, just missing the glistening smear of snail.

'Anfra,' he called. 'My love?' She stopped and turned but didn't answer. 'What's going on? What are you doing out here?'

She mumbled an answer that almost made sense. He

realised she was sleepwalking. A trace of fear cooled the nape of his neck. Then he wondered: is it true that one must never wake a sleepwalker? And if so, why not? Well, what should he do?

They stood in the starlit garden, turned towards each other. Her face glimmered at him blind and pale, strong eyes open and empty. Her beauty struck him to the quick and he was suddenly grateful that he was married to her, however incompletely. It was an aching, painful gratitude that vibrated across his nerves like a bow across the strings of a cello. He reached out to her, calling her name softly, hoping to attract her attention without waking her.

Eugene approached her. Behind her the boughs of the cumquat brandished small thick blossoms, dimly visible; their citrus tang was strong.

'Anfra,' he said, catching her arm, losing his restraint: 'Anfra, please.' Her skin was unbearably smooth and he pulled her close. He buried his face in her neck, in her hair, reached down into her shift, trying to reach more skin, as much as possible. He shivered, grasping for her. She wrapped herself about him, a blossom of thick warm wax.

Eugene Kruger never thought that the first time he made love to his wife, it would be like this: Anfra bound in troubled sleep, her shift thrown over her head, her naked legs forked about a cumquat, the blood of her changed life feeding the earth around the little tree.

When she woke up and discovered herself, she said, 'Oh, Heavenly Father!' Then she sighed heavily and said, 'Oh, my goodness. Oh.' But Eugene didn't know what to say. He was most embarrassed to be seen by his wife in such circumstances. 'I'm sorry ...' he began, but she cut him off softly: 'Don't, don't —' She wanted to say something like: now I am your wife, in flesh as well as in spirit. But she didn't know how to say such words out loud. Besides, she was as embarrassed as he was.

Later she sat up in bed in the dark touching what her husband had seen and touched. One flesh, she thought, one flesh. Her thighs, breasts, haunches, that soft breach — these were no longer her own as far as she was concerned. Joined in holy matrimony, nothing less. But were these parts of herself daubed in God's golden light or tainted by the devil? It was a question she didn't ask, though it entered her mind as a feeling: the sense that something had torn loose and canted over.

Orion soared above, the hunter's admonitory stance warning heaven. Eugene traced it idly as he sat on the rocker on the stoep, smoking his evening cheroot, blowing imperfect rings into darkness. Before Copernicus, he speculated, which part of heaven did the angels inhabit? That particular angel which visited Sarah, wife of Abraham — did it come from red Betelgeuse or perhaps from Arcturus, fourth in brightness? What quarter of the empyrean housed these fiery messengers? Andromeda to the north, Sirius, the Dog-star? Or did the angels circle down from the planets? Would a visitor from Mercury or Uranus confront his wife one day? Bringing what news?

His rocker creaked, the frogs had quietened down. There was a bank of warmer feeling in him inclined to believe in angels, at least on a night like this. The smoke tasted indescribably good tonight. Yes, there was nothing like a cheroot at certain moments, with its overtones of coffee and chocolate and wine burnt off the stove plate. He yawned and stretched: oh, it was good to be a married college lecturer in Franschhoek teaching evolution in this bright modern age.

2

'In the Free State they say it's maize cobs. But I say that stumps of vine make the best firewood for a braai. Gives a flavour to the meat, a perfume, know what I mean?'

Eugene watched blue and yellow flames licking up restfully from knots of vine stock.

'It burns long and hot too. It's not a fussy fire, you can depend on it. Now I say you must do the boerewors long and slow, and the ribs, slow, and things like neck, slow. Then you need durable coals.' He took up a bottle and said, 'I see your glass is empty. More wine?'

'No thanks. I've had enough.'

'Here,' said Koen Sieberhagen, filling Eugene's glass. 'You must drink.'

Eugene frowned, but took a sip. He enjoyed good red wine, but had a moderate nature. Two glasses were enough for him.

'Talk of neck now,' said Koen. 'Have you ever braaied a pork neck?'

'I don't think so.'

'It's delicious! You won't believe it. One day I'll braai you a neck.'

'Oh, it's horrible meat!' exclaimed Anfra. 'Don't listen to him.'

'It's beautiful meat,' he said. 'Lovely and beautiful.'

'Horrible,' she insisted. 'Stinking and fatty.'

'Neck, that's not horrible meat,' said Koen. 'One day I'll get some really horrible meat to braai. One day I'll get a kaffir to braai.' He laughed. 'Maybe I'll get a kaffir's arse. That should be stinking and fatty enough for you.'

'Oh, Koen!' protested Anfra, without heat. 'You get so ugly sometimes.'

Koen brooded over the calm fire, his face turned thoughtful. He shifted the grid about, then turned to Eugene: 'What's this evolution stuff you've been teaching? Is this now a part of science? I thought you were a science teacher.'

'As far as I know, I am a science teacher. What makes you ask?'

'No, nothing. Nothing special.'

'Well,' Eugene ruminated. 'Let me put it differently. You

must have a reason for asking the question. After all, how would you know that I'm teaching the theory of evolution? I suppose people in the town are talking about it.'

'Oh, you mustn't pay any attention to them,' said Koen, obliquely admitting it. 'They're always talking about something. If they have nothing to gossip about here, they'll make it up.'

Now Anfra looked upset.

'But seriously,' said Koen, 'I want to know: what is this evolution stuff? Do you really believe that our grandfathers were apes?'

'Well, since people like Lyell and Darwin published their works you either have to account for their observations, or explain them away if you can't —'

'I'm on your side, you know. I believe in evolution too.'

Eugene was surprised that Koen had any interest in the subject at all.

'Yes,' continued Koen, 'I believe in the evolution of races.'

'Now what do you mean by that?' asked Anfra.

Koen considered and said eventually: 'Some races are more developed than others. It's a question of observation, you know. Anyone who works with kaffirs as I do can prove it. This Darwin chap was right.'

'Well, a number of people have taken this line,' said Eugene, 'but they don't seem to notice that natural selection abolishes the great chain of being ... then again, Haeckel said that except for the ability to interbreed, different races amount to different species ...'

'Ja, of course,' said Koen. 'Kaffirs are a lot more like apes than white men. Like baboons really. They're an inferior species. And when it comes down to Jews — they also have ape-like looks. Different to the kaffirs maybe; they remind me more of chimpanzees.'

Eugene didn't think this was true. 'If anyone looks like a baboon, I do,' he said.

'No, seriously,' said Koen. 'You can mock me if you like.

I've even got a picture of some Jews. I'll show you. Hang on.'

He went into the house. Eugene and Anfra exchanged glances. 'Don't get him started,' she said. 'He's more than half mad when it comes to all this.'

'Come onto the stoep here,' called Koen. 'I've got something to show you. Come into the light.'

As they approached he unfolded a creased pamphlet and found the right page. 'Here. Right here. It's a picture of Jews.'

Eugene and Anfra studied the picture. 'Well,' conceded Koen, 'maybe more like rats than chimpanzees. But it's still evolution.'

The drawing depicted two Jews marked by feral features. One held a bloodstained butcher's knife which he had just stabbed into the necks of about half a dozen beautiful Christian babies, hanging upside down. The other collected their spouting blood in a platter.

'Do you believe this?' asked Eugene, seeing his brother-in-law in a new light. 'What is this document?'

He took the pamphlet and turned to the cover page. It was entitled *My Awakening*. The author was one JHH de Waal, Jr. 'Hardly a scientific document,' he said. 'This is Greyshirt propaganda.'

Koen's face darkened: 'What's wrong with that?'

Eugene said steadily, 'I don't care what your political views are. Just don't make the mistake of confusing them with anything scientific.'

'And what's so holy about science? Maybe a number of people here think that the science you teach is anything but holy.'

'There is nothing holy about science,' retorted Eugene. But he did believe science to be holy. There was something crystalline about scientific thought; it had none of the carnality of religion.

They returned to the fire and stood in an uncomfortable silence that was not broken until the chops were nearly done.

Here was a face chiselled originally of stone. Only the deep and thoughtful eyes were flesh, and the lips which bore the single weakness of a fever blister. But it was worn stone, originally hard and crude, now weathered by age into kinder forms. It belonged to Eben Gerber, the local Dutch Reformed Church dominee. Words of stone too: sun-warmed granite, great dressed blocks of religious truth. 'These things do not change,' intoned Eben Gerber. 'These are the things that last. These are things that endure forever.'

It was warm in the church, with body heat building up inside thick formal clothing, and radiating. 'The Word of the Lord is not a fashion. It is not a fad that people try out and then discard, like so many modern fashions and fads. Yes, the Word of the Lord endures forever.'

The phrases rolled out, rhythmically delivered, calmly indisputable. Anfra rested in their measure and balance. She felt that her soul was made of these words, these ideas, they formed the true substance of her mind. If it weren't for her church and her faith, she would be nothing.

Her hand rested in Eugene's. Here too was certainty. She felt his stable male warmth and knew a different stone, as warm and lasting as the other. If it weren't for her husband, she would yet be nothing. But she was safe; nothing could destroy her husband, nothing could destroy her faith; nothing could destroy the great timeless forms of her religion.

'Here in Franschhoek,' said Dominee Gerber, 'we are like seamen in a small ship. It is a very small ship, I grant you that, but a sound vessel nonetheless. Out there —' he gestured broadly, as far as his arm could reach — 'is the great ocean. And in this ocean are great stormy winds, and fierce currents, and giant waves. There is much danger, much peril out on the seas of the world. But on the ship — on this ship where we sail, this small strong ship — we are sound and we are safe.'

A pew creaked as old Mrs Bester shifted her massive hams, and in the opposite corner a child sneezed. The air in the church lay thick and still.

'Now, by this sea I mean the world of ideas. There are many strange and troubling ideas abroad on the deeps of Satan. And by this ship, I don't mean only the town of Franschhoek. Imagine if you will that this town, this community, this church, is like an ark. An ark bearing the faithful upon the perilous sea of strange and bewildering ideas.'

Anfra, following raptly, glanced at Eugene. He was frowning.

Dominee Gerber took a sip of water. 'Of course you mustn't misunderstand me. I am not saying you should avoid new ideas. This is the twentieth century, of course. This is the age of science, the age of machines, of electricity. The age of the motor bicycle and the telephone. But we must be judicious in the way we treat these wonderful new ideas and inventions, we must be circumspect in our approach, in our understanding of these matters.'

Anfra's mind drifted. She began thinking about the chicken she would make for lunch. Potatoes and green beans? Or roast potatoes? Roast potatoes were so much nicer. She would boil some mixed greens with yellow rice, and serve a tomato and lettuce salad.

The dominee's kind, care-filled èyes licked over his congregation, rested on hers for an instant. She recognised sympathy there, understanding. She felt herself smile.

'We must be careful about what these new ideas, these scientific fashions, might destroy. Faith is such a very strong thing. But in the young — those who are most vulnerable to all manner of cross-currents, and storms of passion, and the battering winds — in the young, faith in the Word of the Lord is often a delicate, a green shoot. A delicate shoot that, at an early age, can be tragically blighted.'

The change was seamless. A dull yellow light had filled the church, bringing with it buzzing fear that drowned all sound, paralysed all other feeling and thought. Anfra didn't know why. Eugene's face had turned to rock, harsh and furious, immobile.

'It is very understandable that a young man, inexperienced, finding his way in his demanding and important profession of teaching, should bring into a community such as ours ...' The dominee paused. He raised his face and looked around the congregation as if to weigh the effect of his words on each soul present: '...certain ideas.'

The words sank and sank. Anfra was chained to them.

'Certain ideas — but let us not judge harshly, my brothers and sisters. There is enthusiasm here, and idealism. We sense it, we feel it, we know in our hearts that there is no malice, there are only the best of intentions. And we must honour and respect one who means well and does his work devotedly and honestly. But —'

His silence had become a vortex. She was lost, spinning down.

Eugene turned to her and whispered angrily: 'Come. I don't have to sit here and listen to this.'

'Eugene, please,' she said in terror, 'please.' She was incapable of walking out of a church; it was an act of blasphemy. She quailed in her seat. He sank back, dull giant waves of fury rocking him.

'I just pray,' resumed Dominee Gerber at last, 'I pray in my heart, and with understanding, and with hope —'

He smiled.

'That my plea be considered. That the imperishable Word of God not be weighed lighter than certain — than certain newfangled ideas.'

A complex sensation rippled through the ganglia of the congregation, chiefly delight at what might become an enormous scandal.

'Let not the inventions of man set aside the Revelation of God!' thundered Dominee Gerber as he raised his hands in blessing.

Oom Deon Viljoen encountered Eugene and Anfra outside the church. 'I believe you've been teaching certain ideas.' He shook his head. 'I think that is a terrible mistake. Look where it got Socrates! No, you must stop this business at once. We can't have ideas in Franschhoek.'

Anfra was too upset to talk. A couple she didn't know came up and shook hands with both of them. They introduced themselves, but she didn't hear their names. They left, smearing their smiles on the air. She caught Eugene saying, 'I must go and speak to that bastard.'

Oom Deon held up his hand. 'No, no, it's not necessary. You mustn't. It's a waste of time to try and convince him of anything he doesn't know already. And bear in mind he's on the college council. It won't do you any good at all.'

'But this is unspeakable.'

Anfra looked about her. The glare had become unbearably strong. There was no shelter. The oak leaves above them shed light, patterns cut in blazing metal.

'My dear fellow,' she heard Oom Deon say. She saw his hand on Eugene's jacketed forearm. 'You know, you can't take this personally.'

'Eugene,' she heard herself say, as if from a distance. 'I must go home and lie down.'

She lay in a darkened room with a cold compress over her eyes for the rest of the day.

In Franschhoek, cicadas lurk in the vines and sing with such shrill ferocity that their sound is painful to sensitive ears. Eugene caught one of these locust-like insects and examined it as he drew on his evening cheroot. Then he let the cicada go, throwing it up into the warm air. It disappeared into the darkness, its wings blurring mechanically. He sat on the rocker, thinking about the dominee's extraordinary sermon. Perhaps there was some truth in what the minister had had to say. He agreed that scientific truth could unsettle fixed opinions. Was it wrong to ask people to abandon views that had endured for centuries? He understood that it couldn't be done without some release of energy, some explosion of heat and dust.

Anfra came out with two steaming cups of coffee and

sat down beside him. He sipped and put his cup down. It was too hot to taste properly.

She touched his wrist lightly: 'Eugene, can I ask you something?'

'Of course, my dear. What is it?'

She looked down as if collecting her forces for an ordeal then said: 'Eugene, I don't mean to pry. Ever since I have known you, I have taken a certain thing for granted. And perhaps that was stupid of me. I had no right to do it.'

'And what is this certain thing?' he asked indulgently.

'My love, I am very serious. Forgive me if I ask something that is none of my business. But it is important to me. May I ask what your views are on the matter of religion?'

He smiled. 'This sounds like you're leading up to a catechism exam.'

She didn't smile back.

'Well, I am not a Hindoo, if that is your concern. I am not a Mohammedan or believer in idols.'

'Eugene, please, this is a matter close to my heart.'

'What exactly do you want to know, Anfra?'

She blushed blurting it out: 'Do you believe in the Lord? And in the Bible? And so on?'

He sipped his coffee again. It was still too hot.

'Well,' he said and stopped.

She watched him. Her lips were parted.

Eventually, he said: 'Probably.'

She closed her mouth firmly.

'Yes,' he said. 'I think I probably do.'

'You think you probably do?'

His cheroot had gone out. He inspected it from various angles, fished out his matches and relit it. He watched as a large cloud of smoke disintegrated.

'It's more complex than that. I no longer believe in the Bible as an historical document. With regard to the creation of the earth and man, anyway. I don't believe that it all took place six thousand years ago.' He smiled again. 'Archbishop Ussher calculated that the miracle of creation occurred about six thousand years ago. Then a chap by the name of John Lightfoot at Cambridge placed the beginning of the world more exactly at nine o' clock on Sunday morning, 23rd October, 4004 BC. He was quite confident about it. I think he understood God to be a kind of English gentleman.'

'Yes,' said Anfra, 'but this Lightfoot must have been in the English church. Does our church believe that?'

'You should ask Dominee Gerber what our church believes. I personally don't. The earth has existed for billions of years. Modern man for scores of thousands. More primitive forms of man lived hundreds of thousands of years ago. No, the Bible is wrong, at least on that score.'

Anfra said, 'I see.' Her lips made a tight compressed line.

For a while there was nothing to be heard except the sound of insects and Eugene puffing at his cheroot.

Dreading the answer, she asked: 'How can you believe in God then?'

He picked up his coffee and sipped. It was too cold. He put it down.

'I believe in the Bible as a moral document. I see it as an account of spiritual truths. Not of geological facts.'

An aura of fear enveloped Anfra, so strong that she didn't quite hear her husband. He stubbed the cheroot out, unaware of the riot of her feelings.

Eugene looked around the classroom: bleak south light falling on desks and books and hands. Ululating dove voices pouring through the sash windows. Suits filled with clean-shaven young men wearing stern expressions.

There was an atmosphere. Nicolas Jacobus Gerhardus Severus Kriegler sat slumped, his head resting on his palm, an accusatory light in his eye. Schuitema's gaze followed Eugene's every movement, his lips thin and compressed as if he expected the lecturer to do something startling, ready to disapprove. Gouws kept his eyes to the desk.

Eugene sensed hidden glee in some quarters, as if he had been birched by Dominee Gerber's sermon, a punishment justified, deserved. He had anticipated this.

'In view of a particular sermon in church yesterday,' he announced, 'which some of you might have heard, I would like to make a small change to our routine. Instead of our normal Friday morning session on evolution, we will discuss the subject today, if there are no objections, of course.'

There were no audible objections. The atmosphere was now so thick one could cut it with a knife.

Eugene ploughed on: 'I would like to step back from the biological details we have been discussing, and look at things more philosophically.'

He picked up a Bible — to the surprise of the class — and read: '...out of the ground, the Lord God formed every beast of the field and every fowl of the air; and brought them unto Adam to see what he would call them: and whatsoever Adam called every living creature, that was the name thereof.'

Eugene closed the book and put it down. 'I'm not going to make a sermon of my own, gentlemen. I would rather talk about the somewhat awkward relationship between scientific and religious thought. I will take what I've just read as a starting point: the story of creation in Genesis that explains how living things came to be.'

Nicolas Kriegler's hand went up. Eugene paused and said, 'Mr Kriegler?'

But the hand went down.

Eugene continued: 'Living organisms were classified by Ray in the seventeenth century, and by Linnaeus in the eighteenth, into groups according to their similarities and differences. But as Linnaeus went on, he realised that the notion of a species was not very clear-cut at all. There were too many exceptions to make a simple rule. This problem had an effect on religious and biological thought, which were not as entirely separated as they are today.

'The creation myth —' Eugene cleared his throat and looked around. 'Let me rephrase it,' he said. 'The biblical account of creation hardly supports the concept of a species. God created lions, shall we say, and Adam named them. But how then does one explain the species relationship between a lion and a domestic cat? Or the structural relationship between an elephant and a coney?

'Despite this absence of scriptural authority, it was assumed by the creationists of the eighteenth century that God had created all the species and genera, all the families of animals, in the beginning. Then the species, it was supposed, reproduced themselves forevermore in exactly the same form in which they were created. But as knowledge accumulated, the extreme variety of animal forms, the absence of clear distinctions in so many cases, had to be explained. How could one relate these complex and confused orderings that were observed in the animal kingdom, these sometimes unsatisfactory groupings of animals, to the divine purpose that is supposed to be at work in the world? Stated differently, what did these complex classifications reveal about the thoughts of God?

'Various attempts were made to answer this question. One such approach was to describe the world as a kind of machine working in a regular manner. The operation of its parts was regulated by complicated but understandable laws. These laws were seen to come from a divine governor. In this view, God had created the world, but through the medium of the natural laws. These laws assisted him, so to speak, in the process of creation. This was very convenient, because the scientist could then continue to investigate the laws of nature while still believing in God.

'The Scriptures declare that God created the world; moreover, that He created it for the benefit of man, who was placed at the pinnacle of creation. So a second attempt to reconcile scripture and biology lay in this direction: to assume that nature was bent to conformity with man's needs.'

'I beg your pardon, Sir?' interjected Willem Janse van Rensburg, an earnest scholar with a round head and perpetually mild expression.

Eugene said, 'According to this second view, the world is a garden designed by the divine gardener to keep man comfortable, happy and well-fed. An optimistic perspective which we could share only with the greatest difficulty today, particularly after such world catastrophes as the Great War and the Depression, or, say, the inflation that destroyed the economies of Central Europe.'

Kriegler's hand went up again.

'Mr Kriegler?'

'I am not sure, Sir, why we are discussing this.'

Eugene made no reply at first. Willem Janse van Rensburg knocked his books off the desk. The doves stopped singing, then their music surged back, liquid and pressing.

'Because,' Eugene said eventually, 'I am trying to show you that views evolve too, as do living organisms. If you follow my lecture to the end, you will see that at first, God was seen to be the almighty Creator; then He withdrew somewhat and became a benevolent governor, or perhaps an intelligent mechanic who loved His machine; then a forgetful watchmaker who wound up His clock and let it run down slowly while He occupied himself with other things; and eventually it was observed that God might possibly be absent, or even dead —'

Eugene stopped. He noticed for the first time that Nicolas Kriegler had gone pale, and that Janse van Rensburg had picked up his books and was standing up. Then the latter walked out of the class, wordlessly, mild as ever. Heads swivelled after his progress, and he closed the door precisely. Eugene blinked and continued his lecture as if nothing had happened.

But something had. Students never walked out of class at Franschhoek Teacher Training College, unless they had been dismissed. As Eugene concluded the lecture, he suppressed an uncomfortable feeling: that a clock was ticking in the machine of the class, that a hammer concealed in the works was drawing itself up to strike.

Autumn is the best time of the year in Franschhoek. The oak and plane trees, the vineyards let loose enamelled leaves, leaves of oxidised metal; long bonfires of scarlet and ochre drift in the gutters. The oppressive heat is over. Relief infects the whole town, young and old. It is so much easier to breathe and sleep and move and gossip; the air at night has a medicinal chill.

In this time of ease, only Anfra slept badly. She was kept awake at night by her fear of what would happen to Eugene's immortal soul. She would be unable to spend eternity with him after the Day of Judgment. She prayed daily and nightly for his salvation and return to belief, but it didn't help her sleep. A new element had poisoned the peace of her marriage, and destroyed every moment she had with him. And then (she tried to suppress the thought, but couldn't) if she had known his religious views, could she have married him? She was sure she would have. She loved him. But then, what of her own soul? Didn't that make her as bad as an atheist herself? She woke up every morning bruised and exhausted, and the rings under her eyes deepened.

Eugene came back from work and sensed something was wrong. He paused at the door; the house was too quiet, as if no one were there. He looked about. There were no visible changes but the house was charged with a feeling of desolation. He opened the door and called out: 'Anfra?'

She didn't answer. Normally there was a hot lunch waiting, together with an animated wife ready to share it with him. But there was nothing in the small dining room, and only a pile of unwashed breakfast utensils in the kitchen.

Anfra was in the bedroom. She was awake, lying against the pillows, watching him silently from dark, sunken eyes.

'Anfra! There you are — why didn't you answer me?'

She looked down. Her hand plucked at a fold in the sheet, plucked and let go again.

'Anfra, what's going on?'

'I'm tired, Eugene. That's all.'

'You're tired?' He found this immensely puzzling. He was seldom tired himself. 'How can you be tired?'

Irritation flooded her: 'It's just the way I feel, Eugene. I don't choose to be tired. I just am.'

Such tiredness was beyond his experience. He said: 'I'll go and make some lunch. What would you like?'

'No. I'll make lunch. It's alright.' She got up and put on her dressing gown.

'No, it's alright,' he said. 'Don't worry. I'll make something.'

'No no, it's fine. I'm not tired. I'll make it, it's time I got up.'

'You don't have to get up if you're tired.'

'I'm not that tired, Eugene, I'm going to make lunch now.'

He put down his briefcase and his jacket and said with what dignity he could manage: 'Thank you.'

He went into the bathroom and washed his face. His reflection glanced back at him, showing its bewilderment.

He sat at the kitchen table, watching her prepare a meal of smoked meat and salad. For the first time ever, he didn't know what to say to her. He didn't know why. He was baffled. His optimism was baffled. He listened to the crisp slicing sound of her knife, the tranquil song of doves, the crack of his knuckles.

She served the meal and sat down at the table with a cup of black coffee. 'Aren't you going to eat?' he asked.

'No, I'm not hungry.'

'Anfra, have you been taking that liver tonic Dr van Aswegen prescribed?'

'No. I can't stand it anymore.'

'You should. You're short of iron.'

'He's a horse doctor. I don't need it.'

'But if you're so tired —'

'I'm not tired.'

To cover his perplexity, he shoveled food into his mouth.

Later he sat at his desk with a pen in his hand and an empty sheet of paper in front of him, trying to plan his lectures. The dense trilling of cicadas formed an arabesque in his mind. He couldn't think. Anfra sat on the couch behind him, sewing, eyes smudged into her pale face.

Silently she watched her husband undressing. He folded his clothes methodically. He was a neat and ordered man. He reminded her of the Ten Commandments, even though he didn't believe in them. She closed her eyes; the sight of him made her weary. His voice came from a distance: 'A hard day, I'd say.' Who did that voice belong to? She didn't know. It said to her: 'What's going on, Anfra?'

Her own voice resounded inside the bones of her head: 'Nothing's going on. What do you mean?'

'This ... all this ...'

Mercifully, his voice stopped. She waited. She realised after a while that she wasn't breathing. Am I dead, she wondered. I can feel the sheets though. They scrape against my skin like sand. She started breathing again. No, I am not dead. I am only buried. Her eyes started open. 'Oh, God!' she exclaimed involuntarily, sitting up in bed.

Eugene jumped.

'I don't know, Eugene, I don't know what's going on with me. I just don't know!'

His frustration boiled over: 'You hardly talk, you hardly eat — Anfra, I don't know you anymore!'

It was the first time she had seen him angry. She was shaken. Her head sagged, and she wept, without resisting it, without a word. Eugene stood naked, arms raised in silent appeal against the sheer unreasonableness of the female cosmos.

This image of her husband appalled her. She was unable to breathe. She called out his name, her voice strangling. He came to her, awkwardly, reluctantly, and held her.

Her head arched back. She had gone deathly pale and the veins in her forehead and neck stood out terribly. It wasn't a convulsion so much as a spasm of violent, unnameable feeling. Then she went limp, and let go a great shuddering breath.

He laid her down against the pillows, where she rested. He wiped her forehead gently with his palm. She took his hand and pressed it against her cheek and said, 'I'll be alright, Eugene. I'll be alright.'

Later in the night, she woke up and clung to him, wrapping her legs about him. He turned around and came into her urgently, almost violently. But it wasn't sex she wanted. She lay hardly moving, her eyes opened — the moonlight falling into the bedroom was fierce, striking dark shadows off the shapes of cupboard and dresser — while he ploughed into her. Afterwards came the bitter realisation that they weren't one flesh after all. The flesh of a man is different.

3

Anfra opened the door to a hesitant knock. A coloured woman stood in the bright morning sunlight, holding a cloth bag. Anfra noted the high cheekbones, the large dark eyes, the lips generous to a fault. She said: 'I'm sorry, I can't help you.'

'No, Madam, Mister arranged it with Mr Deon, my sister works for him, and she said I must come. I'm the maid.'

'Oh, the maid! Of course.' Anfra appraised her in this new light. Eugene had spoken to Oom Deon Viljoen about a maid. Oom Deon had spoken to his wife, who had spoken to her maid, who had recommended her sister. And here she was, a wiry woman with long fingers, and a scarf about her head.

Anfra stood back to let her pass; she walked in with a slouch, an insouciant slouch, but none of it was to be apparent in her speech.

'What is your name?'

'Jolene, Madam.' She pronounced it 'Medem'. She kept her eyes suitably downcast, but Anfra saw the laughter present in the lines of her face, and thought: typical coloured.

Anfra showed her round the house, explaining her duties, instructing. Jolene said little except 'Yes, Madam' whenever Anfra asked: 'Do you understand, Jolene? Do you understand?' Then they retired to the kitchen and Anfra said, 'Make tea for us, will you?'

Anfra sat at the kitchen table and the maid made tea.

'Can you read and write, Jolene?'

'Yes, Madam. I'm even studying a book-keeping course right now.'

Anfra didn't hear the latter information. She said, 'So you went to school?'

'Yes, Madam. I've got matric.'

'That's good. Sometimes I will want to leave messages for you when I go out, and I need you to be able to read and write.'

'Yes, Madam.'

Anfra leaned forward and rubbed her temples.

'What's the matter, Madam?'

'It's nothing, I get bad headaches.'

'Madam doesn't look well.'

'No, I'm not well at all.' She rubbed fiercely, digging her thumbs into her temples so hard it hurt, as if pain could drown out the more severe pain inside.

'What's wrong with Madam?'

'Oh, Jolene. It's nothing. Just a headache.' She smiled wanly but the maid's exuberant presence pierced her like a thorn: a compound of sexuality, health, intelligence.

There was a touch on her arm. She looked up, startled. Jolene was standing above her. 'Can I help Madam to her bed?'

'Please.'

The maid escorted Anfra down the passage. Anfra pressed the back of her wrist against her forehead and winced. Goblin laughter shone out from beneath Jolene's mask of sympathy, ready to disappear at the first hint of a challenge; but if Anfra observed her expression, she didn't comment on it.

As Jolene drew the curtains, three geckos scuttled out and halted as suddenly, a cast of runes. She shrieked as she saw them and Anfra jumped. Recovering from her fright, Jolene laughed at herself.

Anfra called for a cold compress. Then she lay down in her darkened bedroom with the wet cloth over her eyes, dreaming over and over again of a forest fire, while Jolene dusted the house.

When Eugene came in, she was on her knees in the gloomy passage, polishing the floor. 'Good day,' he said. 'I am Eugene Kruger.'

She looked up at him and smiled crookedly; he could see that she was forcing herself not to laugh. She raised her hand to her mouth. Her eyes were wide with the strain.

He wondered what it was about himself that she found so amusing. Frowning, he said, 'You must be the new maid.'

'Yes, Mr Eugene.'

'What is your name?'

'Jolene, Mr Eugene.'

'Welcome, Jolene.'

Then he passed down the passage, and disappeared into Anfra's room.

Later, he asked Jolene for coffee. She brought it to his study and found him seated at his desk, his shirt sleeves rolled up, that frown on his face. She put the coffee down in front of him. He cleared his throat, and she jumped. Her hand covered her mouth again, as if by itself. What is it, he asked himself, that amuses her so?

'My wife tells me you're doing a course of some kind.'

'Yes, Mr Eugene.'

'A correspondence course, I take it?'

'Yes, Sir.'

'Well, that is good. That is very good.'

He lifted the cup of coffee to his lips and sipped cautiously. Then he smiled suddenly: 'It shows you have an active mind.'

She didn't know what to say.

The cup came down. 'Jolene,' he said.

She looked enquiringly at him: 'Mr Eugene?'

He squared the sheaf of paper before him and took a fountain pen out his pocket. What did he want? He frowned at the pen as he unscrewed it. She liked his eyes. They were kind.

He said, 'If you need any help with your studies, please don't hesitate to ask me.'

She thanked him. As she reached the door, he called out, 'Jolene Galant.'

She turned, and he asked, 'Your surname is Galant, isn't it?'

'Yes, Sir.'

'I thought so.' He smoothed the blank sheet of paper in front of him with his thumb.

'Thank you,' he said finally, dismissing her. She went back to the passage floor, her sore knees, the smell of Cobra wax.

In his study, Eugene wrote in his backslanting hand: 'Jolene Galant'. He was puzzled by his own action. Why would he write the maid's name? Moving deliberately, he capped the pen, screwed up the piece of paper and left it on his desk. She was obviously intelligent, he thought. There was something calming about her presence; he felt it in his chest, an opening of the vessels, a clarity that wasn't there before. Perhaps it was the effect of the coffee, which she had made far too strong. His frown deepened: why did he think she was intelligent? There was something luminous about her, he decided. An attractive, luminous quality. He was attracted to intelligence in people, especially in women. Perhaps she was simply luminous and not at all intelligent. But what exactly was a luminous woman? Someone, he supposed, who wasn't perpetually tired. He felt he ought to stop thinking about this matter and unscrewed the cap of his pen again; he had a lecture to prepare.

Jolene was to fit into the household quite comfortably. She slept in her small room at the back, and bathed in a zinc tub which was kept in an even smaller room with a drain set in the floor. She took her meals in the kitchen. She went home at lunchtime on Saturday, and was back at work by seven on Monday morning.

Dominee Eben Gerber wrote to Mr Eugene Kruger, inviting him for tea at the manse on Thursday afternoon. As the letter was addressed to the college, not his home, Eugene assumed that Gerber had something more than the usual pastoral small talk in mind.

He lived in an elegant Cape Dutch building, behind a sweeping lawn and green clouds of weeping willow. As Eugene walked up the neatly kept path, his sense of annoyance grew; by the time he lifted the brass knocker he was almost in a temper.

The dominee answered the door himself. 'Ah, Mr Kruger,' he said, smiling warmly, his eyes cautious: 'I am so glad you've found the time to visit me. We have so much to discuss.' He stuck out his hand, shook Eugene's and said, 'Welcome. Not only to my home, but to Franschhoek.'

'Thank you,' mumbled Eugene, wondering who the dominee was to welcome him to this town. Was it his property?

Gerber ushered him into his cool, pleasantly gloomy study. The shutters were partly closed, keeping out the worst of the heat but not the noise of pigeons and strident cicada.

He offered Eugene tea: 'It has a cooling effect, you know.' He rang a little silver bell. He said, 'I am very partial to my pot of tea,' and laughed gently. 'I must say it is the only positive contribution the British have ever made to our country.'

'Mr Rhodes also brought squirrels,' said Eugene.

The dominee mouthed a syllable: 'Ah.'

The door opened and a maid entered. He turned to her: 'Maureen, this is Mr Kruger. He teaches science at the college. We are lucky to have him.' She smiled, showing naked gums, and smoothed down her apron. 'Bring a pot of tea, please. And some cake if you have any.' She glided out. Then he gathered himself and peered at Eugene from a face of intelligent stone. 'I mean it, you know. There aren't many staff at the college with your qualifications and undoubted expertise.'

'Thank you.'

'Why, I told the rector the other day that he was a lucky man to have you on his strength.' Eugene nodded gravely. 'Speaking personally,' continued the dominee, 'I am quite grateful that you have arrived. There are not many people in a town like this — and it is a wonderful town, please don't misunderstand me, a lovely Christian community — with whom I can share a really *satisfying* intellectual conversation.' His eyes rolled back: 'Mind you, there is Oom Deon Viljoen, and your rector, Dr Lubbe. And perhaps, come to think of it ...'

The voice rolled on. Eugene took out his neatly folded handkerchief and mopped his brow sluggishly.

'...and I was given to understand,' said the dominee, having arrived at a different topic, a delicate one: 'that I was tactless in my sermon a while ago, when I touched on the matter of evolution. The theory of evolution.'

Eugene paid attention. Eben Gerber was looking at him expectantly. He cleared his throat and said, 'Not at all.'

'Please understand that I meant nothing in the way of a personal criticism. But I am concerned —' and his voice deepened, took on a practiced moral weight — 'that the impressionable, ah, the young people —'

Maureen brought in tea and cake. They were silent as she served it.

The door clicked to and the dominee said in sudden

haste, 'But I don't mean to dig up dead cows. I simply mean to say that I hope I haven't ruffled your feathers, so to speak?'

Eugene shook his head stolidly. 'Not at all,' he said. 'I took no offence.'

Dominee Gerber beamed: 'Cake?'

'Thanks. Too hot for cake.' Eugene took out a cheroot and bit off the end. 'Mind if I smoke?'

Gerber helped himself to cake and Eugene lit his cheroot. Then the dominee repositioned himself in his chair and said, 'Mr Kruger, I trust you won't object if I speak to you about something closer to home.'

Eugene gestured with his cheroot: 'Go ahead.'

'Franschhoek is a very small town and things get around. Of course, nobody minds their own business here. But perhaps that is a good thing, if it demonstrates that we care about our brothers and sisters.'

Eugene was frowning furiously. The tip of Gerber's tongue flickered out, licked at dry lips, disappeared. He said: 'Please understand what I am about to say in the light of that brotherly concern.'

'Of course,' replied Eugene, insincerely. He sucked his cheroot, leaned back and exhaled towards the ceiling.

The dominee sighed. If only he knew the young lecturer better. But he squared his shoulders and addressed himself to the question: 'I have been given to understand that Mrs Kruger has been a little under the weather lately?'

Eugene focused on Gerber and said nothing. The dominee ploughed on. 'You know, I can well understand it. A new town, a new community. I blame myself, I have been remiss. I must send my wife round to ask her to join her Bible study group! I wonder why Mrs Gerber hasn't done so already?' He leaned forward and jotted down a note.

Eugene was reluctant to speak. But he dragged his voice out of that well into which it had sunk: 'Yes, she has been quite melancholic. I blame myself —'

'No, no.' Gerber raised his hand firmly. 'She just needs

time. Time to adapt, to her new town, her new role. You mustn't blame yourself.'

Eugene put the cheroot back in his mouth. No smoke. It had gone out. He waved it at Dominee Gerber and mumbled, 'You know we have no children, just the two of us, she doesn't work ...'

The dominee leaned forward, his voice urgent with compassion, and said, 'But it is the burden of womanhood that weighs so heavily ...'

Eugene took him literally: 'Well, we have a maid now ...'

'Excellent!' Gerber leaned back, pleased. 'Support, that's the thing. An extra pair of hands. And I must remember to get my wife to ask your wife to take part in her study group. I'm sure that will be helpful.' He reached out for his notepad, took up a pencil, and then put it down again. He confessed to Eugene: 'I have such a terrible memory, Mr Kruger. Sooner or later I will be senile.' He stared out the window, as if contemplating his blank future. 'Ah yes, the maid,' he said, picking up the scattered threads of his concentration: 'I'm sure that will be a good thing. Most helpful.'

Just then Eugene had a strange feeling, a crawling of his scalp, a prickling in the nape of his neck. He stubbed out his cheroot. 'Smoking too much,' he said. Dominee Gerber smiled and offered him cake again.

Anfra kept track of things in the rambling house through the increasingly cool afternoons, as if her sleeping body were an ear in which sounds and whispers pooled: the scuttling of insects across the floor, the creaking of the ironing board, the scrape of a knifeblade. She followed Jolene's progress from room to room through the rustling of linen or the rhythms of sweeping. Sounds she had no physical right to hear entered her dreams where they were amplified into a kind of explanation or argument: she had to explain Jolene. Why was an explanation necessary? Because Jolene didn't need iron tablets, she didn't need to eat liver or drink stout. Jolene didn't need to sleep in a darkened room every afternoon.

One close Thursday afternoon Anfra dreamt that she was giving birth to a hard porcelain doll and woke up screaming, struggling to tear her way out of the sheet which wrapped about her with malign will, refusing to let go. Jolene burst in and Anfra went very still, panting desperately, her mouth open, stricken.

'Goodness, Madam,' exclaimed the maid, 'I thought there was a robber in the house!'

Anfra sat in the kitchen sewing as Jolene sliced onions, releasing their sharp odour. They chatted quietly, Anfra asking questions about the maid's life and background. Was she married? No, Madam. Did she have a boyfriend? Mischievous smile, no answer. Jolene stopped and wiped her onion-swollen eyes.

'You see, Madam, I'm crying.'

Anfra laughed: 'Not because you don't have a boyfriend.'

And then Jolene cut her finger and had to leave the onions alone. Anfra bound the wound, though it was slight, pressing the long fingers between her own. Her own action surprised her. She let go and returned to the hard chair and her needle.

She was sewing a comforter with a biblical text: "The Lord is my shepherd, I shall not want." Bitterness suddenly clouded her soul. Who was she to say that the Lord was her shepherd, and to advertise it on the wall? She put the frame down and sat very still in her chair, her back painfully upright.

She envied the maid, she realised at last, and her throat ached, swollen with sudden emotion. An absurd thought possessed her: Jolene was able to weep onion tears and bleed; but she felt that there was something inanimate, something waxen about herself — she would melt if it got too hot. Or maybe she would just bend over slowly as candles tended to in the summer heat, and become a stooped old woman long before she was supposed to.

She left the kitchen and lay down in her bedroom. As always, the curtains were drawn. Her embroidery frame rested beside nerveless fingers, trailing its red thread, its bright needle. Soon she rested lightly at the boundary of sleep, growing ever more tired. Her back ached. When Jolene brought in tea at eleven o'clock, she sat up quickly and said, 'I am a camel in the desert,' and Jolene said, 'Yes, Madam,' and left. Anfra sipped hot tea, trying to suppress images of ungainly camel joints, the loose cold meat of herself, absurd lips. The sum of womanhood, the sum of her body. After tea she fell asleep again, sucked down deeper this time, and dreamt that Eugene and Jolene had torn her clothing away in shreds and left her sitting upright, naked, on the kitchen chair. Eugene pointed to various parts of her body with an ebony rod, explaining to Jolene what they were and how they worked. Jolene seemed to know already; her eyes smiled with certainty, she glowed with rude health and self-knowledge. Anfra sewed the label of the dream on her embroidery, the one thing she was allowed to hold: this dream was entitled 'The Anatomy Lesson'.

One evening, Jolene approached Eugene and asked him to help with her book-keeping studies. He consented, and soon it became a routine on Tuesday and Thursday nights: Eugene and Jolene at the kitchen table, Anfra sitting in an armchair placed in the kitchen for her during these sessions. She would knit or sew or read religious literature. After about an hour Jolene would thank Mr Eugene, make a pot of tea and go to her room outside.

When Eugene worked with Jolene, an extraordinary feeling of intimacy overtook him: he could breathe more easily in her presence. She proved to be as intelligent as he had suspected, her mind was quick and supple. There was a stillness in her dark eyes, a depth of observation that impressed him. She was receptive of his teaching, and her voice was pleasing. As they worked he stole guilty glances at her, reminded of his wife's presence by the click of needles or the occasional sigh.

After Jolene left one evening a great silence enveloped him. Anfra felt moved to disturb it: 'A penny for your thoughts?' she asked.

From a distance, after a time, he replied, 'One wonders what she might have been with a decent education.'

'There is a mission school at Pniel,' replied Anfra immovably, as if that answered the question in all respects.

Eugene patted his pocket and took out a cheroot.

She said: 'You're not going to smoke that thing in here.'

'Sorry, dear. I shall take myself and my cigar outside.'

The chill night air didn't deter him. He sat on the rocker, smoking. Soon he was occupied with Jolene again. He had become disturbingly aware of her. The way she stood, the arch of her back, the thrust of her breasts, the shape of her cheekbones, her crude, cheeky grin. He found certain of her features displeasing, on occasion downright ugly. And yet when he surrendered to the impact she made on him as a whole — the word beauty struck him from time to time, though he was suspicious of it.

The rector, Dr Lubbe, sent Mentoor to summon Eugene to his office. His secretary, Miss Belinda de Jongh, smiled sourly as he came in. 'Are you in trouble, Mr Kruger?' she asked.

'Not as far as I know. What makes you ask?'

'Oh,' she said airily. 'Nothing in particular. Excuse me a moment.' She stood up and knocked on the rector's door and went in. Then she came out again and announced, 'Dr Lubbe is expecting you.'

Eugene entered. He hadn't often been in the rector's office. Dr Lubbe tended to be a remote administrator, governing his college from a certain height. The room made an impression on him: mahogany panels, bookshelves lined with thick volumes, maps, a yellowing globe, a glass-topped desk; behind the desk, reflected palely in the glass, Dr Lubbe.

The rector stood up courteously as Eugene entered and gestured towards a chair. 'Good day, Mr Kruger. Thank you for coming to see me. Please take a seat.'

'Good morning, Sir.' Eugene sat down and looked at him enquiringly.

'I haven't had much of a chance to talk with you since you've arrived. Very remiss of me. I trust you're finding your feet?'

Eugene replied that he was. There were no particular problems of which he was aware.

'I'm glad to hear it,' said Dr Lubbe.

Eugene studied him. Lubbe was tall, with thin hair swept across his rounded, balding head, and earnest dark-ringed eyes. He carried himself with a slight stoop. Occasionally, his left eye narrowed convulsively, bringing the muscles on that side of his mouth up in sympathy.

'Smoke?' he asked, offering a yellow tin of Mills Specials.

'No thank you. I'm trying to confine my smoking to the evenings.'

'Good for you. Bad habit.' The rector took out a cigarette and picked up a heavy silver desk lighter. He flicked it a number of times before it would work. 'Wish I could do the same myself,' he said, exhaling in relief. 'I regret that I am enslaved.' Eugene saw the stained fingers.

'I brought you in for a reason, Mr Kruger.' A quick, direct glance, then: 'Let me get straight to it. Your preoccupation with the theory of evolution.'

'Ah yes,' said Eugene, unsurprised.

'There have been complaints from certain students, and worse, objections from parents. There has been unhappiness,' said the rector, 'unhappiness. I pride myself on happy relations in my college ...'

As Lubbe talked, Eugene felt his weariness lifting. He had the strange sensation of loosening from his body, rising out of it — as if he could fly if he chose to. Yes, he was angry. But it didn't matter. He could see the rector with great clarity, his tic, the grain of his skin, the pulse in the vein across his temple.

Lubbe ceased speaking. Eugene gazed out the window, at bare oak branches framed by the sash. In the distance a dog barked, a high cold note.

'How do you respond then, Mr Kruger? What do you say?'

Eugene collected himself. He said, 'I do not regret teaching the theory of evolution, Dr Lubbe. It seems to me a basic part of scientific education today.'

The rector blinked. He flushed. 'You don't regret?' he asked mildly. He leaned forward. 'It's not a question of regret, Mr Kruger. It is a question of confining yourself to the syllabus. There is a syllabus, isn't there?'

Eugene nodded.

'And does the syllabus anywhere mention this question of Darwin and his theory of evolution?'

'No, Sir, it doesn't.'

'Quite. There is also the question of being at variance with the objectives and ideals of a Christian education, do you see?'

Eugene saw. He said, 'I assure you that the syllabus has not been neglected.'

'You are confident this is the case?' asked Lubbe suspiciously.

'Yes, Sir. I have only a weekly discussion of evolution. I wanted to give my class a glimpse of certain important developments in the biological sciences. I'm afraid that, unlike the curriculum, I cannot pretend that science does not progress —'

'Ah yes, scientific progress,' said the rector. The shibboleth hung in the air, exfoliated, frittered away. 'We must keep up with things, we cannot isolate ourselves here. Quite so.'

He stuck another cigarette in his mouth and lifted the lighter, though half the last one smouldered in the ashtray.

'Speaking off the record, Mr Kruger, just between you and me: I personally have no objection. Haven't read Darwin myself, but of course I'm familiar with his views. We must advance.' The new cigarette wagged as he spoke. 'In a balanced way. Have to keep everyone happy, you know. Happy relationships.'

'Yes, Sir.'

Lubbe nodded, blinked. It was a signal that the interview was over, and Eugene rose and left. He wasn't really sure what he had promised, if anything. He wasn't sure exactly what the rector required.

Miss de Jongh looked up from her typewriter. She gave a sympathetic smile, one that spoke volumes, all misdirected. He closed her outer door and turned down the passage, his footsteps echoing off polished surfaces. He was perplexed and angry. He was a reasonable man, but there was one sin he could not forgive: to remain willfully ignorant.

In the staff common room he broke his rule and lit a cheroot. Too clever by half, he rebuked himself, as he stared into the terra incognito he had just negotiated (by omission, by mistake) with the rector.

Eugene couldn't say when or how it had begun. In the beginning, in the vague past, she was the maid. She polished floors and made coffee. She had very little to do with him. He hadn't noticed any change. But somehow, Jolene had begun to saturate his senses. He didn't merely see her, she didn't merely move past him, or bend, or smile, or speak. She now struck against his soul with an intensity that was painful. Was this love? Impossible, Eugene thought. He loved his wife, and that was the natural order of things.

She had invaded his working hours. Bittersweet feelings appeared out of nowhere, an inexplicable and beautiful sense of loss perhaps, or infinite hope promised and destroyed in the same instant, distracting him from the task at hand so powerfully that he might struggle to continue.

She invaded his dreams too. He preferred not to pay a great deal of attention to dreams, especially dreams of this kind. Here a thousand positions were taken up, stories told, lives (all his own) run out to different endings. He woke up in the small hours, weary and drained. And she invaded his movements: he often caught himself walking about in stiff and uncertain movements, his usual energetic stride abandoned, as if he was trapped in an inner vigil.

He couldn't say if she was attracted to him. Jolene usually behaved as a servant: polite, distant, never taking the initiative in communication. But sometimes an impish grin flashed out that burnt a lasting impression onto his soul, though he couldn't say whether the smile meant intimacy or only humour.

Besides, there were unmentionable, unthinkable considerations. Jolene was a maid. He wasn't the sort of man who slept with a maid. If such a thing came to pass it would destroy his career and shatter his marriage, and he knew he was a bad liar. Altogether, he preferred not to think about it. His consumption of cheroots leapt. As autumn turned to winter, he spent more and more time on the stoep at night, smoking and freezing and not thinking about Jolene as much as possible.

He sat on the stoep on one of his Saturday night watches. Anfra had long gone to bed. It had been a day of unexplained silences between them, empty rather than hostile. It was a clear night, and particularly cold because of it. The stars glittered above cruelly. Where was Andromeda now, where was Orion's Belt? He didn't care. The habitual pleasure he took in naming every conceivable part of the world had abandoned him. The garden was silent, without the winter chorus of sand toads to disturb the peace. Only the cumquats flourished, swelling in silent profusion on the miniature tree. His mouth tasted of ash. His life too, he thought. That too was ash. Despair inflamed him. He rose like an old man and felt his way inside, frozen to the bone as he probed his way through the dark house.

He went to Anfra's bedroom, aching with need. As he climbed into her bed, she woke up. She raised her head — yes, he insisted, it was a beautiful head, the correct one — and saw him in the near darkness, found his hand and kissed it. Her sleep-warmed lips were hot against his chilled skin. 'You smell like a cigar,' she said, gently.

'I ought to. I've smoked enough of them.'

To his surprise, she nestled against him. His hand stole under her nightgown and pressed in between her thighs.

'Too cold,' she gasped, but she pressed her legs more tightly over his hand. He pulled his hand away, and rested it on her stomach. Her muscles tightened. But she let him do it. The tempo of his breathing rose and he pressed against her, his cold hands clamping her body.

'Eugene please,' she whispered helplessly, but didn't hinder him.

A strange thought possessed her: what would it feel like to be Jolene in that position? What would Jolene feel? What would she do? Guilt flared up and consumed her. But it was too late. Her body was responding to his, out of control — in a base animal manner, as she rebuked herself later, seeking purgation in the angry white thoughts of the Pauline letters — and then things were beyond reckoning, her body lifted to positions new to her, and her feelings abandoned beyond shame.

Afterwards they lay together silent as snow, both frowning in the dark. She wanted to ask: Eugene, do you still respect me? But she didn't dare. Ironically, he wouldn't have been able to answer her question, he would have felt unworthy of judging the matter. Throughout their love-making he too had imagined: that it was Jolene's more wiry limbs binding his own.

4

There was snow on the mountains above the town, a rare event. It was cold in the classroom. Their breath came out as plumes of frost. Eugene looked out the window, at the bare dripping boughs. He turned back to the class: 'Do you play billiards, Mr Kriegler?'

'No, Sir.'

'Does anyone here play billiards?'

Several hands went up.

'If you strike the ball, Mr Hugo, is its course determined by necessity or design?'

'I'm not sure what you mean.'

'Will the course taken by the ball be determined by natural laws that existed before you struck it? Or will it follow your intentions — in other words, will it travel strictly according to your design?'

Stefan Hugo considered the matter. He was very large, a first team prop forward. 'Definitely design, Sir. I mean, it won't go at all unless I strike it.'

'Does it go exactly where you strike it? Every time?'

Hugo frowned. Then he grinned. 'Most of the time, Sir.'

The class laughed. So did Eugene. Then he said, 'If you chose to make it go straight up in the air, move directly to a position above the nearest pocket, hover for a minute then drop straight down into it — would the ball follow your design then?'

'I wouldn't design to do such a thing, Sir.'

'Why not?'

'It wouldn't work.'

Hugo suddenly saw the point.

'Would you agree then, Mr Hugo, that your intentions in playing billiards must be defined by certain laws — the mechanical laws, for example, that determine the behaviour of a body in motion?'

'Yes, Sir — I would have to agree to that.'

Eugene turned to the class: 'Do we have general agreement, gentlemen?'

There were nods and murmurs of assent.

'Good,' said Eugene. 'Now what if we struck out, as it were, Newton's laws of motion, and replaced them with the principle of natural selection?'

No one answered. Willem Janse van Rensburg's hands went to the books on his desk. He stacked them more carefully.

'Let us assume,' said Eugene, 'that the, ah, Divine Being has created the world according to His sublime and providential design. Let us assume further that He allows this design to work itself out by means of natural laws — such as the laws of motion affecting physical objects, or the principle of natural selection affecting animal life. Could we agree to these assumptions, gentlemen? Are there any objections? Or do you believe that the good Lord personally oversees the course of each billiard ball? Or, for that matter, the adaptation of each species to its environment?'

He looked round for objections. There weren't any. Janse van Rensburg's pale hands left the books and disappeared below the desk; Hugo hunched hugely over his desk; Kriegler's face had tightened.

'If we agree to these assumptions, and I take your silence as tacit assent — we can then proceed to certain questions.'

Eugene paused and peered out the window. A squirrel had climbed further and further down a long, slender bough, until it was clinging to the end, swaying just outside the window frame.

'Natural selection,' he said to the squirrel and the class, 'has otherwise been described as survival of the fittest. So the various species adapt and change.'

He approached the window and opened it to observe the drama more closely. The squirrel was now face down on the last several inches of the branch, which was swinging up and down in response to the animal's careful movements.

'Survival of the fittest, gentlemen, does imply death of the unfit. Considering all the many species of animals — and varieties of man — now extinct, it does seem a cruel way to go about things.' He swung back to the class:'Would you agree that this is something of a conundrum? For a benevolent creator, that is, to allow such savagery and slaughter?'

He looked outside again.The branch was now swinging in a lateral arc as well as up and down.The squirrel didn't seem distressed: just cautious.

A coldness exceeding that of the air had penetrated Eugene. He couldn't quite feel his own limbs. He would have described his state as dreamy if it hadn't been for an extreme and disturbing clarity of mind. 'Not only in the animal kingdom, narrowly considered,' he said. 'When I was a child, the Great War engulfed Europe.The most advanced nations in the world, all members of the most highly evolved race, fought each other for territorial advantage and material resources. Many millions of young men your age died. Over a million in a single battle. It will probably happen again, sooner than you might think.'

The squirrel fell ten feet.The arch of its back depressed as it landed, absorbing the shock, immediately recovering its proud curve.The animal sat up, looked about, hopped off and dug out an acorn embedded in the grass.

'Not merely to allow it,' he said out the window, 'but to make it the very instrument of progress ...'

He turned his back on the window and said loudly to the class: 'What can we assume — from this apparently wasteful and selfish principle of natural selection — about the nature of a loving god? This is the position some of Darwin's friends and opponents found themselves in, you see.'

The coldness Eugene felt was reflected in the stillness of his students. He kept still too, very still. Then he began moving forward, as if on thin ice:'I am not sure, gentlemen, if your present silence arises from hostility to these thoughts, or because I have forced you to some measure of agreement. But I only ask questions. If you apply your minds, you are sure to discover a way out of this dilemma.'

Not entirely honest, he thought. He hadn't found a way out of the dilemma himself.

Warming his fingers over a cup of tea in the common room after the lecture, he reflected on the expression on Nicolas Kriegler's face. It was a picture of anxiety, and cynicism: the mechanism of natural selection was something Kriegler understood well but deliberately kept secure from his inner life, an aqua regia stoppered in a fragile glass vessel.

Snow still frosted the mountains on the northern side of the town, though the weather had improved. The little party abandoned the stoep and gathered under a pale sun: Anfra and Eugene, Koen, Oom Deon and his wife Lettie, and Anfra's father Barend, who had left his farm in the depths of winter to visit his daughter on her birthday.

Jolene Galant had been asked to stay in this weekend to help with the party, with serving and cleaning up afterwards. She brought the coffee and the cake and stood in the background in polite attendance.

Eugene had bought Anfra a Kodak for her birthday. He made everyone stand up, then rearranged their chairs for a formal portrait. They sat down again and composed themselves for the photograph.

Posterity shows Anfra seated in the centre of the group, her hands resting on her lap, her mouth stretched into a fragile smile. On either side sit the men of her family. Koen is stern and erect: if action is to be taken, Koen is the man to do it. Barend is stern too, but sunk into the puzzled indifference of the near deaf. Deon and Lettie Viljoen flank the group. Lettie is a figure of disarranged kindness and Deon smiles cleverly, filled with the secrets of his long memory. Eugene is not in the picture.

He stood holding the camera, turning it about, testing

the view through the frame. He cocked the shutter lever and after squinting up at the sun, adjusted the aperture. He pointed the camera and urged everyone to smile. Everyone smiled, stark shadows painting out their eyes. Eugene was dissatisfied. He noticed Jolene, who had just brought a fresh pot of coffee. He asked her to stand in various positions while observing the effects of sunlight and shadow on her face.

When he found the right place, he lifted the camera to his eye again as a test and composed her in the viewfinder. She smiled uneasily. The privacy and exactness of that frame had an unexpected effect, releasing something he had forbidden himself to experience: the violence of his feeling. He was struck, with the impact of a musical chord ringing out, by a further discovery: he was in love with Jolene. She was more beautiful to him than his wife, and far more alive. A harsh sweet vitality poured from her image, an intensity that burned without consuming itself. And was it sympathy he saw as she peered back at the camera? His hands were shaking, with relief, with fear and sudden excitement. He breathed deeply, inhaling the soul before him, and took the picture.

The family group had fallen silent; their jocular comments on his photographic efforts had ceased. He turned to them, alarmed. Could his sudden perceptions have become visible, flowering in the air above him in full view of his family and friends? Was the miracle of his love exposed? They were immobile, unreadable, as if they had become a photograph themselves or a carving that holds time back for a while, a solid coloured one. Was it judgment in their eyes?

He turned back to Jolene Galant. She was still holding the tray. 'Has Mr Eugene finished?' she asked. 'Can I put the coffee down now?'

'Yes, thank you, Jolene,' he said. He pointed to her: 'That is the right place to sit for the picture.'

With humorous groans and exclamations the group

lifted their chairs and rearranged themselves.

'Join us, Eugene!' cried Anfra gaily, waving him nearer. 'Let Jolene take the picture!'

But he wouldn't let go of the camera. He took the picture himself.

The party stretched on into the late afternoon. They moved inside the house, where Jolene had made a fire, and Eugene opened a bottle of wine. Barend Sieberhagen sat in the corner armchair, nursing a neat brandy.

Deon sat beside him and said primly: 'I fear that we are heading for troubled times.'

Barend ignored the remark.

'The storm clouds are gathering over Europe, do you not think so, Mr Sieberhagen?'

Mr Sieberhagen failed to express an opinion.

'But I am inclined to optimism, despite the worst of contingencies. I once saw a plaque in a church in Yorkshire, which I took the trouble to memorise. It goes something like this.' He cleared his throat and intoned: '"In the year 1652 when throughout England all things sacred were either profaned or neglected, this church was built by Sir Robert Shirley, whose special praise it is to have done the best things in the worst times and to have hoped them in the most calamitous." 1652, you see. I thought it was a most coincidentally propitious moral for our country.'

Barend stared straight ahead, giving little sign that he had heard.

'I fear that in the event of war, Mr Smuts might not prevail upon Mr Hertzog to support England. If there is one thing that will destroy this land,' warned Deon, raising his hand in trembling prophecy, 'it is our great love of the *insular*. I think that is our *Germanic* legacy.'

Barend sipped his brandy. He stared sourly at his glass, swirling the liquid.

Deon's outstretched hand had become a raised finger. He shook it and said, 'There are a great many virtues in the

Germanic side of things. But if our government leans in Mr Hitler's direction, it will be a catastrophe for everyone, I can tell you that quite confidently.'

Expression slowly accumulated in Barend's eyes and gathered to a point. He lifted his head and said darkly: 'You can't trust him. That Smuts is a two-arsed jackal.'

When the lamps were lit and the curtains drawn, Oom Deon gathered his wife. They said farewell and departed, Deon complaining that by now he was so dizzy with coffee that he would have to lie on his bed and keep very still until things settled down; he was positively liverish.

Eugene was quiet over the evening meal, indifferent to the sluggish flow of Sieberhagen conversation. His desire unleashed at last, he followed Jolene's every movement as she served, painting over with his gaze the smoothness of her skin, her high cheekbones and full lips, the hidden calm insouciance. Then he caught Koen's eye resting on him speculatively. Shame prickled through Eugene and he tried to confine his attention to its proper and loyal orbit, which was naturally the body of his wife.

Directly after supper Anfra went to bed, complaining of tiredness. Barend had fallen asleep in his chair; Koen rescued from his father's hand a glass of jerepigo that was about to tip over.

'Well, old chap,' he said, 'the men are alone.'

He drained his father's jerepigo, then held out his own empty glass to Eugene and shook it. Eugene poured for him. A single snore escaped Barend, then he settled back into the long sibilant rhythms of his breathing. A fresh log hissing on the fire let go a battery of explosions. Eugene lit a cheroot and leaned back, inhaling gratefully.

'Nice bit of tail you've got there,' said Koen, gesturing in the direction of the kitchen. 'Well, reasonable, I'd say, for a hotnot.'

Eugene released cigar smoke and said nothing.

Koen brooded over his wine, his head slumped forward.

He was deep into his second bottle of red wine but the only visible effect was paleness, and his eyes were slightly out of kilter. As if in bored confession, he said, 'It's difficult sometimes, Eugene. You're a man of understanding.'

'What is difficult?' asked Eugene dryly.

Koen still looked down into his wine, reading the secrets of its dark surface. 'Women,' he said. 'Sometimes a man in my position has advantages which he finds difficult to avoid taking ...'

'Really?'

'I mean as a single man on a farm. No one can see what you do — you're alone with the labourers, and they don't count for much. You realise after a while that you're in a tremendous position of power.'

Eugene listened as Koen talked, his eyes narrowing. This was a side of his brother-in-law he hadn't encountered before; he had seen Koen only as a shrewd buffoon.

'Your married man, now, he has considerations that I don't have. Obligations. Or if you're courting a white woman, you know — I don't have to labour the thing to death.'

'What are you getting at, Koen?'

Though Eugene could see where this was going, a morbid interest made him prod for details.

Koen drank deep and said: 'I take what I need. A couple of shillings, half a crown will sort out any injured feelings ...' He turned fully to Eugene, his expression frank yet bruised with guilt: 'Sometimes, only sometimes, I have to hurt one. Not a little, but just enough. In fact I prefer it that way. Maybe they do too. No one has complained so far. But to be honest, that's probably because the supply of labour on the market is generous, and I don't see things changing.'

He let go a shuddering breath, then stretched out his glass again. Eugene stood up, poured for Koen, fed and poked the fire. Light from the blaze fell across Koen's sharp features. Eugene was reminded of something predatory but immobile, like a stuffed leopard or the cold eye of a pike in oils.

'This is the difficult part,' said Koen. 'The really difficult part. Love is one thing, and *poes* is another. You take what you must, but you feel dirty afterwards. And you realise, sometimes you just have to be dirty. A man is a dirty thing.' He waved his hand sloppily, and Eugene saw from the movement how drunk he really was. 'You can take your white woman and her wedding dress, and her trousseau, and the minister's speechifying in church and your honeymoon, and your roses and all. But underneath that — underneath *everything* — at the heart of — it's just *poes* you're after. White or coloured, whatever you like, it's only *poes*.'

Eugene didn't reply. He didn't know how to reply. The fire crackled furiously and the heat drove him back to his chair. He tried to deal with the fact that his brother-in-law had just admitted to raping a number of women. Did this make him evil? Eugene thought so. Koen was staring into the fire expressionlessly, as if he had said nothing remarkable. The pile of flesh in the corner that was his father Barend had sagged deeper down into sleep, the breath whistling in and out. Was Koen nothing but evil? Eugene didn't know. He picked up his cheroot and stoked it to life again, contemplating his own worth: was he any different in kind, if not degree, from Koen Sieberhagen? Again, he didn't know.

Long after Koen had gone, Eugene sat on the stoep, wrapped in a greatcoat, smoking. It was his turn for a splitting headache. His head was split by a question: if there were no God, or no God concerned particularly with the business of men, what was the measure of evil? And if the mechanism of natural selection had replaced the scale of good and evil, what was Koen? He was troubled by the only answer he could find: nothing but a particularly well-adapted predator, of course. Something to be admired for its fitness.

Barend returned to the Free State, and Anfra saw him off tearfully at the station in Paarl. She was depressed for a few days, but then came an invitation from Mrs Gerber, the dominee's wife, to attend a Bible discussion class for married women. The group met every Tuesday evening.

They were currently reading 1 Corinthians and measuring their own Christianity against St Paul's counsel. They tended to find themselves wanting, but not greatly. One could be virtuous and modestly guilty at the same time. Although Mrs Gerber was an imperious woman, she had adopted Anfra as her special interest, gave her attention and encouraged her. The others in the group followed Mrs Gerber's example.

Anfra heard her own aspirations described and echoed in the discussion: of family life, the woman in a Christian home, the spiritual dimensions of a wife's love. They would sit about the gleaming table in the warmly lit and heavily furnished dining room of the manse. The older women aired their rich sure contralto voices. In this established and kindly place, in this moral light, Anfra felt safe. She began to feel at home in Franschhoek, at last.

Eugene pushed his chair back abruptly and stood up. His heart battered at the walls of his chest and he found it difficult to breathe. But he was no longer able to shape his own actions, and emotion flooded through the broken earthwork of his resistance: relief, guilt, dread, a great nervous excitement.

He stood behind Jolene, resting his hands on her shoulders. She looked up uneasily from the cashbook, letting her pencil fall. She leaned forward, perhaps in unquestioning submission, and he slid his hands down to her breasts. She closed her hands over his and said, 'No, Mr Eugene! We can't do this!' But she didn't remove his hands and her voice was lilting, teasing. Her shoulders suddenly shook and a surge of alarm took him. Was she distressed? But alarm gave way to chagrin as he realised she was shaking with laughter.

She brought herself under control and asked: 'What does

Mr Eugene want?' She let go one of his hands and his chagrin turned to shock as she reached behind her and grasped him strongly. 'Does Mr Eugene want this?' She pressed tighter: 'Is this what Mr Eugene wants?'

He shook his head but knew that he was lost beyond hope of recovery. He leaned over her, his mouth sinking down to her neck. Then he raised her from the chair and turned her round to him. He looked down on her smiling, anxious, insolent face.

She disengaged and protested, 'No, Mr Eugene! We can't do it in Madam's house. It's not right.'

He cleared his throat but couldn't speak, gestured towards the kitchen and led her through. They paused at the back door and looked out cautiously, because the moonlit yard between the kitchen and her outhouse room was open to the street. Eugene almost drew back at that point; but it was a short street used only by its few residents, and was clear of traffic. Again, he hesitated. Jolene looked back at him questioningly, and he knew there was no going back.

They entered the dark, small, poorly ventilated room. As its musty atmosphere enveloped him, something wrenched loose in Eugene, and he was speechless with the violence of this loss: it was not righteousness he felt being stripped away so much as his self-control, the sovereignty of his reason. He had passed a threshold; now he was part of that long, anonymous, squalid procession of men who sleep with the maid. This time he didn't falter, but closed his eyes — as if in prayer — and accepted this new description of himself humbly.

She undressed without ceremony or remark, and went on all fours before him. She looked back and said, 'Come now.'

This position created a certain difficulty, as his legs were so much longer than hers. 'Mr Eugene is so tall,' she remarked sympathetically as she adjusted her position and guided him in. The frigid air goosepimpled her skin, the cold light turned it to textured marble. He reared over her, fashioning from the two of them an absurd mythic beast; pewter moonlight from the high window lit the frost that poured from his mouth. She held the position but when she rested her head on the pillow, her body rounded and mobile, animal and sculpture at once, shivering yet warm to the touch, he released himself convulsively and it was over.

They lay together under her blankets. She had no sheets. The bed was warm with her smell. Eugene didn't know how to talk to her. Was she the maid, or his lover? Neither description was correct. When she pressed herself hard against his quiescent manhood, he said, 'Jolene, I think Mrs Kruger will be back from her Bible study quite soon.'

He had an urge to tell her that he loved her, but he didn't. He felt it would be a shameful thing to do.

He stood up and began pulling up his clothes.

'I must get my things from the house,' she said, meaning her cashbook, her ruler and pencil.

He finished dressing, sat down to pull on his shoes, and then he was ready to go. 'You'd better stay here,' he said. 'I'll fetch your books. It will be safer.'

Jolene lay in her bed and said, 'Thank you for the lesson, Mr Eugene.'

He nodded. Then he left, closing the door softly behind him. He came back soon afterwards and tapped on the door. She opened it and he silently gave her the cashbook and stationery. She looked up at him. He was unable to read her expression, though abundant moonlight fell on it. Her eyes were coal-dark, a mystery to him, and her mouth seemed bruised. He gently brushed his hand against her cheek. 'Thank *you*,' he said hesitantly, 'for the lesson.' Then he left.

As winter deepened, Anfra's happiness grew. In consequence of the Bible class, she was invited to tea as much as twice in a week by the various pillars of Franschhoek society (it was a society consisting mostly of pillars). She didn't have much to say in these lounges dense with chiming clocks and glistening furniture, among the matrons of the town; she affected a listening presence which worked, carried by her impressive eyes and still hands, her few nicely timed comments. But she really did listen, attentively, and gathered a simple wisdom that had been sorely lacking. Other women also felt ambivalent about their husbands; they could gauge and express that distance without a criminal sense of betrayal; they could laugh at their men without great disaffection or cruelty. Quite apart from any understanding gained, her inclusion in society was itself a relief. Taken out of her isolation, she put on weight, slept less in the afternoons and better at night; the rings under her eyes diminished, though she still suffered oppressive attacks of fear.

There was a further improvement in her life, something she only realised gradually. It was brought about by a change in Eugene's behaviour. Although he had never bothered her about sex with great frequency, he had become less demanding, less intense — in fact, almost cursory. That too was a relief for Anfra, a gift she never questioned, just another of the many vagaries of men. What little thought she gave the matter yielded this explanation: her husband had grown more accustomed to the married condition, and so naturally expected less of it.

After breakfast on a Sunday morning, Anfra made ready for church. As she applied her lipstick, it occurred to her that Eugene was still in his pyjamas. She turned round from the mirror and said, 'My dear, have you noticed the time?'

'It's eight-fifteen.'

'We'll be late for church if you don't get up and get dressed. You haven't even shaved.'

'I don't think I'm going to church this morning.'

Anfra turned back to the mirror and applied one more dab. His words sank in, and she kept dead still, her hand arrested. Slowly, slowly, it sank to the glass top.

'I see,' she said carefully, not sure if she should ask why. She decided not to, and opened her powder compact. A fragment of her face stared back from the little mirror in the lid.

Eugene offered the information, his voice neutral: 'I've decided to withdraw from the church.'

She closed the powder compact, forgetting to use it, and turned back to him.

He raised a hand, forestalling her: 'I've got nothing against the church,' he said, 'and this doesn't really change anything. It's just that ...'

He stopped. He knew why he wasn't going to church, but couldn't tell her. He felt it would be hypocritical to sit in a church on Sunday while he was fornicating with the maid on Tuesday. And then he wasn't sure whether he believed more in original sin or natural selection. He wasn't sure if there was any difference, or if the processes of nature amounted to God or were something different. He didn't believe that sitting in a church with an ignorant preacher at its helm would advance his understanding of matters at all. Finally, he wasn't sure that God visited the church at the same time as the rest of the congregation, at nine every Sunday and again at six. It seemed too pat, too orderly an arrangement for the Creator (if He existed) of such a riotous complex as the natural order.

He realised that she was still staring at him anxiously. He shrugged and said, 'It's just something ...'

Anfra was struggling to form words. With regrettable clarity, with sadness, Eugene realised that he didn't understand his wife at all.

He completed his sentence: 'Something that happened.'

She was a face on top of well-chosen clothing. He feared that she would become a broken face. He struggled to keep things normal, to keep things the way they were. He even said it, hastily: 'Anfra, nothing has changed — you just go to church on your own, that's all. I'll walk there with you if you like.'

How absurd he sounded to himself! Could she hear the lie that clanged so loudly in his own mind?

Anfra gave him a small and reassuring smile and said, 'No need, my husband. I will go to church by myself.' She got up, went to him and kissed his brow. 'I'll pray for you too.'

He thanked her politely. She completed her preparations and went out.

After she had left, Eugene wandered round the house, from room to room. Only the lounge, Eugene's study and two bedrooms were furnished; the house was large and rambling, with several more rooms untenanted and unused. They were swept occasionally, but smelled permanently of dust. He had made love to Jolene inside the house a number of times, on the odd afternoons when Anfra went out for tea. They did so because it was too dangerous to cross the yard to Jolene's room in broad daylight. Jolene, however, would only do it in the unfurnished parts. The furnished rooms were distinctly 'Madam's house', and that contravened some odd, private ethic of decency. When Anfra went to her Bible class at night, Eugene and Jolene had the comfort of her bed; otherwise it was his greatcoat thrown on a cold wooden floor. But wherever their coupling took place, it was hurried and taciturn and uncomfortable, and so all the more intense for Eugene.

Now he wandered through the house, from his wife's carpeted domain to his lover's bare country, trailing a cloud of cheroot smoke. He came to rest in the small attic room that overlooked the side street they feared. This room too was unfurnished; he had taken Jolene here as well, seated on an empty packing crate while she sat on his lap and wrapped her legs around him. The crate had left a splinter in his left buttock, but he couldn't ask her to remove it; the task was somehow too mundane and too intimate at once. He couldn't ask Anfra either, and so he had to leave it there, to work itself out. It was still there now, causing a trivial but annoying degree of pain.

He stared out of the window, seeing nothing, his mind crowded with impressions of Jolene's body. He was far from realising — it didn't have any significance for him at all — that he didn't know who Jolene was either. She was a closed book to him.

There were many kinds of hats in church. The woman sitting in front of Anfra wore an objectionable one. It contained too much fruit, linen shaped into marzipan balls. The hat filled Anfra's vision. Something about it repelled her. As if there were a praying mantis stalking that colourful jungle, retreating suddenly behind a fabric plum whenever she looked up.

Beyond the hat, to the side, very small, high up in his distant pulpit, stood Dominee Gerber. A maroon and tasseled piece of velvet draped over his podium bore a legend in gold letters: SO SPREEK DIE HERE. She often wondered why the name of the Lord was mentioned twice.

At a certain point in the sermon she reached out automatically for Eugene's hand, but of course it wasn't there. When she closed her eyes and couldn't see the hat, she could hear the dominee better, each word ringing out clearly; but she couldn't combine the words together in any way that made sense of them.

It wasn't dread that filled Anfra, it was sadness. She would have Eugene throughout her life, and that was well and good. Her loss lay thereafter: she would have to face eternity without him, a more absolute divorce than life could cause.

She stared down at the cleanliness of the book open on her lap. Where she would find the steel she would need in her soul to endure the long ages of heaven? The congregation rose to sing a hymn. She remained seated, unaware of their movement. Her vision blurred with tears as she mourned the spirit of her still-living husband.

5

Aclatter of stones on the roof brought their sex to a halt. Jolene looked up in fear. There was a voice in the streets, coarse shouting, running footsteps.

'What did he say?' asked Eugene urgently. 'Did you hear that? What was it?'

The maid shook her head in the near dark. 'I don't know,' she said.

'You're trembling,' said Eugene softly.

'Mr Eugene must go.'

'I need to finish!'

'Please, Mr Eugene. Please.' Her voice was rich with fear, with pleading.

He couldn't disengage. 'They're gone now,' he said. 'I must, I have to —'

And he did, holding her down. Everything was dark for him. He became a creature of dread, blind with surpassing need, excitement perverted by her fear. Her eyes were wide open, her head turned to the side as his urgent movement continued. Then he was done.

'This is trouble, Mr Eugene, this is serious trouble.'

He knew she was right, but he didn't say anything. He just rubbed briefly the warmth of her body — which part exactly, he couldn't say — slowly collecting himself. He was frowning into the shadowy silence of her room, considering what the incident meant.

She huddled under the blankets as he slowly got dressed. She said again, 'This is bad, Mr Eugene. Please, Mr Eugene must go now.'

Eventually he said, 'You're right, Jolene. We will have to be more careful.' He was dressed now, standing, looking down on what he could see of her shape. But he knew that it didn't matter any longer how careful they were. This clatter of stones, these shouts of crude anger in the streets, had left a slope of ruin in the near-dark more visible than any object there. He left, closing the door quietly.

As he stood in his own back yard, taking his bearings, rage slowly accumulated. He walked to the fence and looked up and down the street. There was nothing to be seen, no movement, only the bulk of the mountain to his left — a more concentrated darkness — and the empty street to his right.

He went into the back yard, through the kitchen and into the living room. Anfra was there, reading. Eugene stopped. He was filled with his anger, the shock of Anfra's presence, the warmth and movement, the shapes and scents of sex with Jolene. It was too much to carry. Gradually he realised that Anfra had said something.

'What?' he asked.

'Where have you been?'

'I was out — walking. I went for a walk.'

Was that suspicion on her face?

'In this cold weather?'

'In this cold weather — it doesn't bother me, you know that.'

Her expression wasn't suspicious. It reflected an inner distance from him, something as unprecedented as suspicion would have been. Eugene couldn't tell the difference. His guilt was too great, the outrage of almost being caught.

'Why are you home?' he asked carefully. 'I thought you were at your Bible class.'

'Mrs Gerber was taken ill and we decided to end it. Mrs de la Bat brought me home.'

'Nothing serious, I hope?'

'No, I don't think so.'

He didn't want to approach her. He was still filled with Jolene. It would have been too flagrant a thing.

'Well —' he said.

Anfra nodded, and picked up her book again. Eugene went to run a bath.

Later that evening he sat on the stoep, as was his habit, wrapped in a greatcoat, smoking a cheroot. He allowed himself to inspect his feelings at last: guilt, fear of disclosure, a horrible sense of things unraveling. He still had his anger and determination, but knew he had no real control over events. It was a disconcerting experience. He stayed there long after he had ground out the stub of his cheroot, painfully aware of the two women in the silent house behind him.

As Eugene was walking home from work, the rhythms of an idling engine interrupted his musing. It was Koen Sieberhagen in his dusty black Chevrolet, cruising up beside him.

'Hop in,' said Koen, 'I'll give you a lift.'

Eugene smiled. 'No thanks,' he said, 'I prefer to walk.'

'Hop in anyway. I want to talk to you.'

Eugene got in. They set off smartly down the main road. As they passed the turn-off to his house, Eugene glanced at his brother-in-law. Koen's expression was forbidding.

'Where are we going?' asked Eugene.

'Just down the road a bit. I need to chat to you, in private.'

Eugene took out one of his cheroots. 'Smoke?' he asked. Koen declined. He lit it and waited to see what Koen had to say. But his brother-in-law said nothing until they were beyond the town limits. Finally, Koen said, 'Look, old man, I don't like interfering in someone else's business.'

So, thought Eugene. It comes to this. He released a cloud of smoke, filling the car with it.

'I'm not a hypocrite,' said Koen. 'And I don't like interfering —'

'You've said that.'

Koen looked at him stubbornly, squinting through the smoke. 'I think you know what I mean,' he said. 'I myself don't care what you do. But people are talking, and this is a very small town.'

Eugene stared out at the passing landscape, considering his options. Eventually he said, 'They're talking about nothing.'

'That's what you say — but I've learnt by now that where there's smoke, there's often fire.'

'Maybe,' said Eugene. 'If they're talking about someone else's fire they're talking about nothing.'

Koen took an exaggerated patient breath: 'Look, Eugene, I've been in this town longer than you have. I know the territory here. If this goes on —'

'There is nothing going on.'

'Alright,' said Koen, 'I'm not arguing with you. I accept what you say. There's nothing going on. But I care about my sister.' His face was tight with anger. 'I don't give a damn if you want to hurt yourself and destroy your career. But I don't want Anfra to suffer the damage while you dip your prick into some —'

He stopped. Silent rage had enveloped both men.

Koen pulled the car over, and tried again: 'Eugene, you're my brother-in-law. I have some respect for you as a person. And between you and me — I know my sister, I know her better than you think — I'm sure she's not easy to live with —'

'Now you're *really* not minding your own business.'

Koen set the car in motion, turning laboriously in the narrow road. He brought it to a halt on the opposite verge, shook his finger at Eugene and said, 'I don't care what you do. But if this carries on and word gets out — and it will get out — I will not let you do this to my sister. I will not let you do this to my family.'

The finger slowly subsided. Eugene absorbed with contempt Koen's unflinching righteousness, his arrogance.

'You'd stop at nothing, wouldn't you?' he asked quietly.

Koen made no reply. There was cruelty evident in his bearing, and determination. It was answer enough.

'There's nothing going on,' said Eugene finally. 'And this isn't your business.'

'I've warned you,' said Koen dully. 'If things go wrong.'

He jerked out the clutch and they shot back into the road to town.

As he did all his guests, Dominee Gerber offered Anfra cake and tea. She accepted, but quite obviously didn't feel like eating. She toyed with her cake. She sipped tea delicately.

'What can I do for you, Sister?' he asked finally, his voice dipping into the heavy music of ministerial intonation.

'I've asked to see you, Dominee, as I have been deeply worried — I have a great concern — my husband that is, I don't know how to explain this —'

As she stuttered on, his expression plumbed the depths of gravity. She grew breathless with anxiety. But she managed to define her problem at last and Gerber's expression lightened. 'Ah,' he said almost happily: 'now I understand. It is the materialist attitude, the conviction of godlessness, yes —'

He was relieved because rumours about her husband were circulating, and he was glad not to have to confront the terrible thing they whispered. He closed his eyes briefly and prayed: may the frailty of ignorance protect her.

'I share your concern,' he said ponderously. 'It would be a great pity if a man as talented as —'

He suddenly was unable to remember the name. He looked at the pale expectant face, the dark eyes. Her lips opened slightly.

'As your husband — if such an intelligent man were to become an atheist. Yes, a great pity.'

She leaned forward earnestly and said, 'Dominee, there is another thing troubling me. I have done everything I can. I am not a highly educated woman, and I cannot discuss intellectual matters with him. I believe that my attempts have made things worse.'

She was very troubled. He waited for her to continue, but she didn't. He was not an unempathetic person. He could feel the emotional weight that she carried, that she presented. He was also a practised minister: he understood that she wanted to leave some of the burden with him. 'Would you like me to speak with your husband?' he asked.

'I would be grateful.'

'Do not expect too much,' he warned her dryly. 'There is nothing more pernicious than an atheist. They stick to their views with exemplary faith, in my experience.'

This wasn't entirely true. Dominee Gerber had far less experience of atheists than he implied. Even the most downright evil people he had known were God-fearing. It didn't really matter though: he had no intention of talking to a man like her husband, a man at the centre of such deadly rumours.

Still her dark eyes demanded.

'Is there anything else?' he asked tiredly.

'Yes, there is. There is something else, but I'm not sure if I can speak about it.'

'You could try. It is good to share even the most bitter of our burdens. If we don't, they can work on us like a poison, undermining even the most faithful and cour- ageous soul.'

She couldn't look directly at him: 'Dominee, what will happen at the end of our lives, if Eugene remains like this? If he is still lost, lost to God —' She finished with difficulty: 'and I am a believer?'

Deep and earnest sympathy passed across the dominee's face. One might even call it a tragic expression. 'Sister,' he replied, 'The ways of the Lord are mysterious, and you must never give up hope. You are young, both of you — you have long lives ahead — who knows what might happen in the course of the years?'

He tried to read her as she sat before him, so filled with an intimate pain, with a spiritual yearning she couldn't share.

'Never give up hope!' he added fiercely.

'Thank you, Dominee,' she replied uncertainly. She still couldn't meet his gaze, and doubt flooded her every movement.

'Come, Sister, let us pray together.'

He closed his eyes and prayed at length for her and the husband. She thanked him, clasped his hand and left.

Alone in the study, he ate her slice of cake. Sometimes you can do nothing to help a person, he realised sadly, except pray.

A warm Sunday brought Anfra and Eugene out into the garden. She laid out a platter of cold meat and salads; he poured himself a glass of beer, a small sherry for her.

'Do you remember when we first came here, to the house?' she asked him. 'The garden looks better, don't you think?'

He smiled at her: 'I still think it needs a few ducks and a bantam or two.'

'Well, we have a tortoise now.'

A geometric tortoise had indeed found its way into the garden and was sometimes seen wandering around like a small and bewildered boulder.

'I have no problem with the tortoise,' he said, 'but they're not very productive. I'm not fond of tortoise eggs, and they don't eat snails.'

Anfra closed her eyes and drank up the sun. Winter rains had swollen the stream, and its music was strong and clean. For no good reason — this beautiful morning, the sherry perhaps — she could lay aside the dark questions of eternity that had so depressed her. 'Do you remember the day we arrived?' she asked out of her sunlit darkness. 'I was silly enough to faint.'

'You were indeed silly,' he said. 'I had to carry you over the threshold.'

There was silence. Then: 'Eugene, if you want to get some ducks, I don't really mind.'

He glanced at his wife, at her pale face turned up to the sun. She was beautiful, he thought, surprising himself. But what was the link, what connected him to her? What really lay behind that pale mask he caught himself admiring? An honest curiosity moved him and he rested his hand on hers. Anfra opened her eyes and turned to him. Her searching gaze caught him by surprise.

But he held it and asked, suddenly grinning, 'Do you remember our night under the cumquat tree?'

She smiled back. 'Not much. I was sleepwalking, remember. Then you just about raped me.'

'I don't rape you often enough.'

Her smile grew frail, and faded. She turned back to the sun, closing her eyes again. He withdrew his hand.

After a while, she said, 'We live in a beautiful country, Eugene. Sometimes I think this is heaven on earth, or a type of earthly paradise, I should say. When I think of these mountains all around us, and the autumn leaves, and the bare beautiful trees —' She stopped.

After a while she said, 'A good husband too. I have everything. I should be very happy with all these blessings around me.'

The irony of it branded him.

She struggled on: 'But it's not really paradise here. I'm not that big a fool to think so.' The words closed down on her, her mind went numb. 'We might as well enjoy the sunshine,' she said finally, 'while it lasts.'

So she did, closing her eyes, resting in the warmth, hoping the light would speak to Eugene for her and say the things she couldn't.

Early spring brought with it a second warning. A note was delivered to Eugene's classroom summoning him to the rector's office. Belinda de Jongh was waiting for him with an arch smile. 'Go right through, Mr Kruger,' she said. She swiveled after him inquisitively. At the rector's door he turned to look at her. Her lips compressed primly and she swiveled back to her typewriter. He went in.

The rector was bent over papers. He pretended for a while that he didn't know Eugene had entered. Eugene refused to pretend that he was still outside. He waited.

'Ah,' said the rector, looking up. 'It's you. Take a seat, Mr Kruger.'

'You wanted to see me, Dr Lubbe?'

Instead of replying, the rector looked abstractedly round his desk. 'Cigarettes,' he muttered under his breath. He lifted and dropped several piles of paper.

'Cigar?' asked Eugene.

'No thanks.' The rector patted his pockets. His left eye twitched. Finally he said, 'Look, Mr Kruger, an upsetting thing.'

Eugene raised an eyebrow.

'This evolution business. Inevitable, I suppose.'

Lubbe opened the top drawer on his left, slammed it shut, opened the one on the right. 'Ah!' he exclaimed, relieved. He held up a yellow tin of cigarettes. His hand shook as he struggled to open it. He calmed down visibly as he put one in his mouth. 'See the lighter anywhere?' he asked, cigarette wagging.

Eugene took out his own and lit up for the rector, who inhaled and released a long plume of smoke.

'Ah,' Lubbe muttered, squinting and twitching. 'Enslaved, you know. Bad habit. Can't give up.'

After a few more draws, he said, 'I've been forced into this. It's become a chorus, an absolute chorus. Do you have any comment, Mr Kruger?'

'Well, Sir,' said Eugene cautiously, 'perhaps if you could tell me more about — whatever it is?'

'Yes, of course,' said the rector, pursing his lips as he spoke. 'There is to be a disciplinary hearing. You will appear before the full council.'

A feeling of weariness and distaste passed over Eugene.

'You have been accused of teaching a programme that is offensive to the community, offensive to the ethics, one might say, of this college. I think the term unchristian has been bandied about. Here it is, I have the document.'

The rector looked for it on his desk. He sifted through various piles of paper but was unable to find it. He went to the door and asked Miss de Jongh to search the filing cabinet.

'I'm sorry,' he said, returning. 'Don't know where the thing is.' He sat at his desk, hands clasped, waiting for his secretary.

Eugene couldn't tell whether he was apologising for the loss of the missing document — the charge sheet, he thought sourly — or for the situation itself.

'The father of one of our students wrote to the chairman of the council. Now that happens to be Professor Beyers of Stellenbosch University. Beyers then came to me, and regrettably, I had to tell him what has transpired. Namely, that I had warned you to, ah, desist in this teaching. I made my feelings clear, as you will most certainly recall.'

'I'm not sure that I do —'

'Oh, yes,' interrupted the rector testily, 'I called you in and expressed my disapproval; I left you in no doubt at all.'

Eugene thought otherwise but saw no point in argument. No matter what he said, Lubbe would insist that he had taken a firm stand.

'Who was it?'

'I'd rather not say.'

'Kriegler, no doubt.'

The rector shook his head hastily. 'No, not at all. Someone else.'

Miss de Jongh entered with the missing document and handed it to Lubbe. Then she walked out. On impulse, Eugene turned round and looked at the door. It was still slightly open. As he watched, it travelled the remaining distance and clicked shut.

He took out a cheroot, lit it, and scanned the document. He quickly reached the essential passage, written in fine legalistic style:

That the person aforementioned did wilfully teach, contrary to the regulations of the Council and Governing Board of the

Franschhoek Teacher Training College, and contrary to the express instructions of the rector of the said instance, Dr Albert Lubbe, a certain theory or theories that denied the story of the Divine Creation of man as taught in the Bible, but did teach instead thereof, that man is descended from a lower order of animals...

He read it again more carefully, scowling and puffing his cheroot.

'This is a farce,' he said eventually.

'No, not at all. I cannot describe it as a farce, by no means a farce. You are young in education, and no doubt you will learn that in a certain community — rightly or wrongly, Mr Kruger, I make no personal judgments — in any given community, particularly in a rural one, you can only push things so far.' The rector's apologetic manner had become spleen. 'There is always bound to be a reaction. You dare not impose your will in certain areas. You have to treat the religious convictions of your students with respect.'

'That's hardly the point! I don't agree that I imposed anything —'

'No, let me finish, Mr Kruger, allow me that much —'

Lubbe went on, Eugene's own anger grew. As if from a distance, he watched the rector's mouth moving.

He interrupted again: 'I don't recall you saying anything like this in our previous meeting, Dr Lubbe.'

The rector blinked, offended: 'I most certainly did, Mr Kruger. Perhaps I didn't express myself quite as strongly. But there was never any doubt about my position. It was clear as a bell.'

Eugene studied the tip of his cheroot. 'I see,' he said.

The rector looked at him owlishly. A wave of scorn lifted Eugene. He wanted to laugh, angrily, contemptuously. The cheroot tasted of turpentine. He reached across and stubbed it out in the rector's ashtray.

Dr Lubbe leaned back and took a deep breath. He lit a another cigarette, and looked at the younger man with genuine regret: 'I am sorry this has come about, Eugene. If

I could have avoided it, I would have done so.'

So the meeting ended. Eugene's long legs took him rapidly to the door. As he went out he caught Miss de Jongh scuttling back to her chair.

Eugene pushed his plate away. 'I've been accused at last,' he said. 'It was a while coming... it was inevitable.'

Anfra held her fork in mid-air, motion arrested. 'Accused of what?'

'Of teaching the wrong thing.'

The fork made its way to her face. She chewed and swallowed. 'I suppose,' she said, 'it's the theory of evolution again.'

He nodded.

She looked down at her plate as if studying her stew. 'Why?' she asked eventually.

Eugene considered. So much rested in her one-word question: why did he have to teach the theory of evolution? Why was he accused of it? Why did it matter? Why couldn't he just teach the sort of science that people in Franschhoek expected him to teach? Why was it necessary to change everything, to break things that had lasted so long? Why did he have to darken the image of God?

Bitterness overwhelmed Eugene. Not because of the enquiry, but because his wife could not support or even understand his position. He knew he shouldn't blame her. She was quite limited, he realised — recognised wearily, with resignation — a product of her upbringing. But he did blame her. It crept through his resistance then, to wonder why he had married her. The question filled him with pain.

'What can I say?' he replied. 'I must teach the fruits of enlightened scientific investigation, that is what any teacher of science must do. That's all. It's quite obvious.'

She looked at him doubtfully. Nothing was obvious, not any more. 'What does it mean?'

'I will have to go to a special council meeting. They will

accuse me of teaching a false unchristian dogma. I will defend myself.'

'What will you say, Eugene?'

He shrugged. 'I don't know. I will wait to hear what they say first.'

Her dark eyes studied him, trying to probe the mystery that her husband had become, trying to understand the damage he had caused their lives. 'What have you done, Eugene? You could lose your job, you know.'

'Possibly. I don't think so, they really don't have a leg to stand on. I've covered the syllabus thoroughly. I've had no definite instructions not to do this, whatever Lubbe says, and they will be hard put to find any real regulations forbidding it. None in writing. But it won't do my career any good, I'll grant you that.'

When supper was finished, Anfra rang her bell, a brass bell cast in the form of a bonneted maiden in petticoats. Jolene entered and began stacking the plates and dishes on her tray. Eugene watched her intensely; she avoided his attention.

After supper he followed her to the kitchen. He peeled an apple slowly and watched her as she worked. He lounged against a dresser in the kitchen proper; she was in the narrow scullery, washing the dishes. She tried to make nothing of his presence. She looked at him only once, a glance that he took to be yearning.

He approached, leaned down and kissed her neck.

She shied away: 'No! Mr Eugene!' she whispered urgently. 'Madam is in the house.'

'She's going out tonight, Jolene.'

The maid said nothing and carried on washing up.

'I need you, Jolene. I want you tonight.'

She shook her head sullenly. 'Mr Eugene can't come. It's my time.'

His eyes narrowed as he stood behind her, looking down from his height. He didn't believe her. She had avoided him since the stone-throwing incident.

'I see,' he said. Then he left the scullery and went out the back door into the garden. He listened to the loud music of the stream, the night song of the crickets, and tried to find peace. But he felt feverish and dissatisfied, bitter, cheated. He made his way to the stoep and sat on the rocker, staring blindly into the night. He knew the names of many stars, but each of these was a fact, a label that was mostly empty — containing only a wavering, easily extinguished point of light — no divine intelligence. He recalled sitting in the same spot a lifetime ago, wondering about the angels. Where in the sky were they quartered now? They had brought no messages for him in the past season. God had confined them to barracks, forbidding any contact with teachers of Darwinian science.

After Anfra had gone out, he made his way to Jolene's room and knocked softly. She opened the door a few inches and looked up at him. The candle-lit room behind her seemed a haven. He could smell tallow, and her own earthy fragrance. But her face was hardly visible with the greater light behind it, and he sensed something forbidding about her.

'I need you, Jolene. I want to come in.'

She shook her head. Her lips — what he could see of them — were maddeningly full. He leaned forward and kissed that darkness. Her mouth was soft and warm as always, but closed to him.

He pushed the door open, easily brushing her out of the way.

She watched him, startled, cautious, still silent.

'Please,' he said, taking her shoulders in his large hands. 'Don't look at me like that.'

When she spoke at last, it wasn't in the voice of a servant: 'This must stop, Mr Eugene.'

He bent down and kissed her neck, her face, wrapping his arms about her, almost bruising her back and ribs. She pushed him away strongly, struggling to get out of his embrace. He was too powerful for her. She went limp and sagged against him. He took it for capitulation and partly released her, brushing his hand across her face gently.

'I love you, Jolene,' he whispered. 'I really love you. I don't know how or why, but no one — not even my wife —'

He never completed his sentence. They made love after all. Later, drained and withdrawn, he realised the truth: that Jolene hadn't participated in the act. Eugene preferred not to think about the implications. He had an extremely hot bath and went to bed early.

The disciplinary enquiry into Eugene's teaching was held on the first Monday of the spring recess. He was called in to face five distinguished men of the college board. The chairman of the governing body was Professor Etienne Beyers, formerly of the law faculty of a nearby university, now retired. He was a very old man with creased parchment for skin. Beside him sat Chris Hugo, breathing heavily, a farmer and lay preacher whose shrewd, obese face floated above his strained suit. Next to the farmer sat Louis Visagie, one of the town's two butchers, a thin, dry man with a large moustache. On either side of the group were Dr Lubbe and Dominee Eben Gerber. The table sported a cloth for the occasion, and a bowl of flowers was placed squarely in the middle, partly obscuring the chairman.

After a lengthy prayer — in which Dominee Gerber appealed for wisdom in this weighty matter, summarising the issues neatly for the Almighty — Professor Beyers peered round the bowl of flowers at Eugene.

'I shall begin this hearing, Mr Kruger, by reading the charge against you. I do so with a heavy heart, deeply aware of the burden the Lord has placed on me to judge this matter. Now, Mr Kruger, I trust that you understand why you are here and what is the objective of this proceeding?'

'I understand the objective of this proceeding, Professor,' replied Eugene, 'but I am not at all sure why I am here. I do not understand why this proceeding is necessary in the first place.'

'I shall read the indictment to you,' said the chairman. 'Perhaps that shall clarify your understanding.' He read the indictment. 'What do you have to say, Mr Kruger?'

'To my mind, Professor, creationism and evolutionism are contradictory views. I have come to believe that they are irreconcilable. And yet there are thousands, perhaps millions of sincere Christians who see no contradiction at all. I would say that a necessary conflict arises only between evolutionism and a fundamentalist understanding of the Bible.'

Mr Hugo's stout fingers pushed away the papers in front of him. He leaned forward and said, 'I can tell you what the contradiction is. It's clear to any man of understanding, Christian or heathen. Your true Christian believes that man was created from on high, but people like Mr Kruger here believe he must have come up from below, from the lower — the lower order that is — of animals. That is the difference.' He leaned back, the sound of his breathing filling the room.

'Thank you for clarifying the matter, Mr Hugo,' said Professor Beyers. He pushed the bowl of flowers aside irritably and turned to the Dominee: 'But what does the Christian believe, Dominee Gerber? What is the position of the church on this matter?'

Gerber looked uncomfortable. 'As far as I know,' he said, 'the Synod has not made any decision on Darwinism, on this vexed question of evolutionism.' He shifted in his seat, warming to the topic: 'But in my own view, this notion that we are descended from baboons and so on is a typical expression of liberalism.'

The professor nodded sagely.

'I would have to say,' continued Gerber, 'that if evolution triumphs, gaining ascendancy over the souls of men, Christianity will go to the wall. Not at once, of course, but bit by bit. The two cannot exist side by side. They are as antagonistic as light and darkness; as opposed as good and evil. We must cleave to the Bible, and draw our knowledge from that source.'

'Pardon, Mr Chairman,' said Dr Lubbe, twisting his neck uneasily: 'do you think we could give the meeting permission to smoke?'

Professor Beyers peered at the rector's twitching eye and smiled thinly: 'I think we must keep the seriousness of this procedure in mind. I rule that those who wish to smoke may indulge their need at the conclusion of this meeting.'

The rector looked upset, but said nothing further.

'What do you have to say to that, Mr Kruger?' asked the professor.

'Well, Dominee Gerber might cleave to the Bible and get all his knowledge there, but then he will soon run into trouble. Consider the whale that swallowed Jonah —'

'It was a fish,' intoned Dominee Gerber. 'Jonah 1-7: "Now the Lord had prepared a great fish to swallow up Jonah. And Jonah was in the belly of the fish —"'

'Thank you, Dominee,' said the chairman. 'Mr Kruger?'

'Do all of you present believe that a man lived inside a fish for three days and survived? What kind of fish could swallow a man whole without destroying him? A specially prepared fish? If it was such a fish, what happened to its descendants?'

'I can believe that as well as I can believe in the other miracles!' testified the farmer Hugo, his voice ringing with conviction. But now he was behind the bowl of flowers which the chairman had displaced. In his agitation, he almost knocked it over; only Louis Visagie's hasty action brought it to a trembling stop.

'Gentlemen,' interjected the butcher impatiently, releasing the vase. 'This is neither here nor there. We are not here to consider the Bible. We are here to consider whether young Kruger taught evolution instead of the story of creation. Now there is no doubt about it — he doesn't deny it and if you ask him, he'll admit it straight away. So the next thing we have to consider is whether it was in breach of college regulations, or whether it was a breach of instructions from Dr Lubbe. That's all there is to this thing.'

'I take your point,' said Professor Beyers, 'we must confine ourselves more exactly to the topic. Now what regulation has Mr Kruger contravened, Dr Lubbe?'

The rector cleared his throat noisily. He was badly in need of a smoke. He raised a pamphlet with shaking hands and read out slowly and distinctly: '"The Franschhoek Teacher Training College strives in its educational task towards the scientific preparation and general development of the student with regard to subject competence, vocational fulfilment and commitment to service, which schooling stands squarely within a Christian perspective and values." That is from our prospectus, which we send to all the parents and students.' He looked round at his fellow judges uncertainly. 'It's not exactly a regulation, but it's from our prospectus.'

'Hell, now,' said the butcher, 'does that say exactly you can't teach evolution? Sounds pretty vague to me.'

Dr Lubbe opened and closed his mouth like a goldfish. He waved the pamphlet in Eugene's direction, but had nothing further to say.

'Well then,' asked the chairman, 'what about your direct instructions, Dr Lubbe? What about that?'

The rector's eye was twitching furiously. He gestured towards Eugene. 'I told him not to,' he said. 'We discussed it. I told him not to.'

The heads swiveled back to Eugene.

'We did discuss it,' said Eugene carefully. 'But I wasn't sure what Dr Lubbe wanted me to do. I thought he did disapprove, but then he didn't expressly forbid it.'

'Ah,' said Professor Beyers, 'Dr Lubbe's word against yours. A most unpleasant impasse. Could you excuse us a moment, Mr Kruger?'

Eugene went outside. It took considerably longer than a moment. Nearly two hours later he was called in again and judgement was delivered.

Anfra was waiting for him. She was pale and seemed disturbed. His own smile was haggard as he said, 'I suppose you want to know how it went?'

'I have something to tell you, Eugene,' she said distractedly. 'I have some important news of my own.'

He was too excited to hear her. He took out a cheroot and said, 'I was severely reprimanded. Not for teaching evolution. For not heeding the rector's instructions. I was also told to stop imparting this hellish theory with immediate effect.'

He bit off the end of the cheroot. 'Lubbe almost died, from lack of tobacco. The chairman wouldn't let him smoke. I must say I felt a measure of sympathy for him — I could have used a smoke myself.'

With an effort, she brought herself to respond. She said almost mechanically, 'I'm glad, Eugene.'

He stuck the unlit cheroot in his mouth. It wagged as he said, 'Never heard so much nonsense spoken in my life.'

Her reply seemed to have no bearing on his conversation: 'And Jolene didn't turn up this morning. It is most inconvenient.'

He saw her clearly for the first time — saw that she was shaken, her hair subtly awry, her movements unsteady.

'Anfra, are you alright?' he asked. 'What's the matter?'

'I said that Jolene didn't turn up this morning. It is particularly inconvenient in view of — in view of what I have to tell you.'

It seemed to Anfra that he wasn't listening.

'Yes,' she said insistently, 'I have something very important to say, to tell you. That's the thing. I have some important news —'

He was still absorbed by the fact that Jolene was missing. He raised his hands to his face and turned away slightly as he lit the cheroot, masking himself.

'Perhaps she has a cold,' he said, from behind clouds of foul-smelling smoke, 'and stayed home for that reason.'

Anfra shrugged.

'And what is this important news?'

She approached, took his free hand in hers and looked anxiously into his eyes: 'Eugene, I am pregnant.'

Cold shock rolled over him. But he pulled her to him and embraced her. 'Well done, my dear,' he said, the gravity of his voice disguising his confusion, 'Well done indeed.'

She leaned into the warmth of his body, into the simplicity of touch, and rested there. 'You don't mind, do you?'

'Anfra! How could I mind?' he said heavily. 'This is cause for celebration!'

'If it's a boy, would you mind very much if we called him Sybrand? After my grandfather on my mother's side, Oom Sybrand van Jaarsveld of Ladybrand?'

'Of course we can call him that,' he said, 'if it's a boy. I don't mind at all.'

She couldn't see his face, which was just as well. He didn't know if Jolene would come back or not. But his eyes were bleak as he contemplated what should have been obvious from the beginning, something that was written into the structure of the affair: an empty future.

Jolene

Franschhoek, 1937/Paarl and Cape Town, 1996

1

'Teboso!' I shrieked, putting down the phone. 'I've found her, I've traced her!' He looked up from his book, wincing, I think at my voice, at my intensity.

'Found whom, Jessica?'

'Jolene Galant! They've found Jolene Galant! Oh, Teboso, I don't believe it.'

'Who is she, who are "they" that found her, and why does it matter?'

'The woman, the missing link! She was my grandparent's maid. She's alive still, in an old aged home in Paarl. She was there all the time —'

'Ah, the maid,' he said sourly. 'The so-called maid. Interesting connotations in it.' He picked up his book again, muttering almost inaudibly: 'Milking a cow, no doubt, the maid. That cow with the crumpled horn.'

'She was there, right there when I visited Vredehof, the retirement home in Paarl. Can you believe it? Her married name is Cornick, we just didn't know it was she.'

No reply. He was back in his book.

'I'm going to see her on Saturday, Teboso. Would you like to come?'

His only reply was a grunt. Slowly, resentment at his rudeness built up and crawled into every space in my body, into my teeth, into the proteins of my fingernails.

She was very old, and had no teeth. The flesh of her lips was sunken, invisible drawstrings of age crumpling her lips into a puckered purse. It was hard to imagine her as the sleek desirable woman smiling out of the photograph I possessed.

Now her hard consonants, her plosives whistled through the crack between her gums and came out fricative. I often had to ask her to repeat herself, and had to repeat myself loudly too, because she was nearly deaf. For the sake of fluency or at least economy I won't try to represent all the sounds of our dialogue, nor those whistled and bellowed requests for reiteration or greater volume; but interviewing her was a strain.

We sat in her bedroom, on a bed each, uncomfortably. It was a two-bed cubicle, separated from the long dormitory of which it was part by low divider walls that stopped half a metre short of the ceiling. There was no door into the cubicle, only an opening guarded by a cheap print curtain hanging from a cord. I tried not to think of all the burping and snoring and farting that would flood the air every night in this long gallery, this mustard-painted necropolis.

'Why do you want to interview me?' she asked suspiciously.

'I'm writing a history of my family,' I said desperately. This was not the first time I was trying to explain my motives. 'It's for the university, Mrs Cornick. We have to interview old people — senior citizens — like yourself, to find out about — you know, what things were like then. When you were young.'

'Why are you asking *me*?'

I didn't really know anymore. 'Because you were there,' I finally said.

She nodded sagely.

I seized the opportunity: 'You can help me with your memories of the time. To make the history more real.'

I realised that she was still nodding, like one of those kitsch nodding dogs my parents used to have on the rear windscreen ledge of their Wolseley. I wanted to laugh at her, badly. I suppressed it, but she must have seen whatever traces of amusement were left peeping from the corners of my eyes, crackling from my frizzy hair.

Her head came to a halt, of itself apparently. Then she

chewed at her gums, masticating her words before spitting them out. I was torn between impatience and dreadful laughter, a nervous reflex I suppose. I was terrified it would escape in an embarrassing shriek.

The mouth came to a halt. She opened it and spoke: 'I don't mind.'

'Do you mind if we do the interview in English? I think better in English, somehow.'

She shook her head and said, 'No, I don't mind that. I speak English also.'

So the interview began.

'I believe you were employed by my grandparents, Eugene and Anfra Kruger? Is that correct?'

'Yes, that is correct.'

Then silence. As the pattern recurred, as I watched the little spindles of the recorder turn, I realised she would have to be drawn out, question by question. It was daunting. How does one build up a history, even part of a biography, question by question? Where do you begin? What about the question you might miss, the one that fixes the centre of events?

'Let's take it from the beginning. How did you feel about your new job? What was it like working for my grandmother?'

'Times was hard, Miss Jessica. I was lucky to have a job. It was the war years then, and nobody had a job, you see.'

'Please call me Jessica. Are you sure? During the Second World War?'

'Yes. Because of the war, you see. There was no money, and no work.'

I decided to leave aside the question of the period. 'Okay, it was during the war. What were your impressions — what did you think of my grandmother — of Anfra Kruger?'

'Your grandmother was very nice. She was a lady.'

When a woman of about ninety says the word 'lady', it means something different. I sensed a complex of values in her tone I couldn't quite grasp.

'A lady? You say she was —?'

The gums, those lips went into a spasm of self-discovery again. I had to look away. Then she said, 'Yes, she was a lady. She was very nice to me.'

'So she treated you well, as far as you were concerned?'

'Yes, from the beginning, she was always very nice to me.'

I thought I should try to make things concrete if I could — after all, doesn't history lie in the details? 'Well then,' I said, 'do you think you could remember your first day at work?'

She smiled and shook her head, obviously amused at the lunatic nature of my request.

Here is a possible beginning: Jolene walks down the long main street of the town in autumn. Leaves the colour of hoepoe and kingfisher, fires stained scarlet and ochre, drift into the gutters and choke the water courses. A sunlit tide, a second atmosphere of spores rises and falls in the breeze, spreading through the negative spaces of plane tree and willow, poplar and elm. The town of Franschhoek breathes more easily today, knowing that the suffocating summer heat is nearly done.

At last, there is the house. She stops at the gate, impressed by the rambling structure, the stream and the garden rich with insect song and the odours of humus and decaying wood, the neglected fruit trees live with birds weaving through their branches, ruining the plums. The gate creaks open at her touch; though she is apprehensive, she saunters down the path, her soul resonant with birdsong, with the hues of this beautiful morning.

Anfra Kruger — 'Madam' to Jolene — took her in. It was cool in that interior. Anfra showed her round the house, explaining her duties and conditions of service, instructing. The passage was broad and dark, some of the rooms were unfurnished. So much space, Jolene thought, so many empty silent rooms — too much space for only two people.

Anfra showed her a study, a spartan room with a neatly kept desk, a clinging smell of cigar tobacco. The feeling in this room was different, bouyant and clear.

'My husband's workplace.'

As she backed out of the door and closed it she brushed against Jolene, dry silk against flesh.

They returned to the kitchen where Anfra requested a pot of tea. Anfra sat at the table while Jolene made it, covertly watching her quick movement, feeding on her vitality.

'Can you read and write, Jolene?'

'Yes, Madam. I'm studying a book-keeping course right now. It's a correspondence course.'

Anfra didn't seem to hear this. She asked, 'So you went to school?'

'Yes, Madam. I've got matric.'

'That's good. Sometimes I will want to leave messages for you when I go out, and I need you to be able to read and write.'

'Yes, Madam.'

Anfra leaned forward and rubbed her temples.

'What's the matter, Madam?'

'It's nothing, I get bad headaches.'

Jolene silently passed a cup to her new employer. She stood at the dresser awkwardly, waiting, unsure.

'Pour for yourself, Jolene. Don't be shy. You can sit down here at the table with me.'

The maid poured her own tea, adding sugar and milk. When she turned round again she saw that Anfra was breathing rapidly through pale, slightly parted lips. She looked distressed.

'Is there anything wrong, Madam?'

Anfra shook her head; she had gone white as a sheet. Speaking reluctantly, an admission dragged from her by some inner violence, she said, 'I suffer these dreadful attacks, Jolene.'

'What sort of attacks, Madam?'

'I don't know what sort they are. They are attacks of fear or sickness, I can't say. And then comes a most tremendous headache.'

Jolene helped Anfra to her bedroom. They walked slowly, as if Anfra were an old woman; they were about the same age, not much more than twenty. To Jolene's touch, holding one arm, the other round her shoulder, Anfra's body was strong and light, despite her mysterious affliction.

She looked up gratefully as Jolene settled the coverlet, pressing a fluttering hand over the maid's. 'Thank you, Jolene. Now if you will just draw the curtains for me ...'

Jolene tugged the curtain. Three lizards fell writhing out of their seclusion behind the fabric, scuttling away under the dresser. The women screamed, both of them, a soprano chorus of terror. They looked at each other — Jolene's hands pressed against her cheeks — and burst out laughing.

'I'm so scared of those things, Madam.'

Anfra turned and rested on an elbow, tears half of laughter, half not, trickling down her cheeks, her eyes fixed to the spot where one of the lizards had thrown off its tail. The ejected organ writhed about itself, a thing whole yet disturbingly incomplete, fascinating and horrible as it slowly ran down, the tip beating against the carpet with decreasing energy until it couldn't anymore.

'So much like myself,' she muttered tiredly.

'Beg your pardon?'

Anfra looked up sharply: 'Do you sometimes feel, Jolene — do you sometimes feel that you're not really alive?'

'No, Madam, I never feel that.'

She lay back on the pillows, still pale, despite the isolated pink spot on each cheek. She was three colours — pink, white and black — a painted doll.

In the kitchen, Jolene shivers: the house aches with the white woman's loneliness, crawls like a feverish skin with the passion of her slow, detailed drowning.

Very well. After several more questions I concluded that my
grandmother was 'nice'. She was a 'lady', she was 'good' to
Jolene Galant. That was all I could elicit from my source.
What could I learn about class relations from this muteness? What political lessons? Only one thing filled my
mind, and that was a growing weight of disappointment.

'What about my grandfather then? What was he like?'

Slow as the minute hand of a watch, a thin smile
appeared on her face. She nodded again in silent agreement
with her own thoughts. 'Yes, your grandfather,' she said, her
voice giving 'grandfather' such substance, such egg-yolk
richness that I could have plucked it out of the air and
painted it on my notebook. She paused, reflected again:
'Yes, your grandfather.'

I took a deep, deep breath and let it out slowly.

'Your grandfather,' she said, 'He was a nice man. He was
very good to me. He was now a *gentleman*.'

The first time Jolene sees him, she nearly bursts out laughing. She is on all fours in the passage, polishing the floor.
The door opens and a tall figure comes in from the glare.
She thinks immediately of a heron or crane as it takes tow-
ering delicate steps through the swamp, its wings stretched
out wide.

'Good day,' says the crane, 'I am Eugene Kruger.' She is
unable to speak. She can't risk it. Her ribs strain, she presses the back of her hand into her mouth.

Frowning, he says, 'You must be the new maid.'

'Yes, Mr Eugene,' she replies, her voice quavering. He
leaves her and goes down the passage. She remains on hands
and knees, head hanging down, slowly releasing her threatened hilarity. She sits back against the wall and laughs at
last, quietly and helplessly, till the tears run.

He asked her later to bring a cup of coffee to his study.
She made the coffee and brought it through, placing it gingerly on his desk. He cleared his throat; she jumped.

'My wife tells me you're doing a course of some kind.'

'Yes, Mr Eugene.'

'A correspondence course, I take it?'

'Yes, Sir.'

'Well, that is good. That is very good.'

He lifted the cup to his lips and sipped cautiously. Then he smiled: 'It shows you have an active mind.'

An active mind. What did he think she was? Just the maid, of course. But the smile took her by surprise.

His cup clinked down on the saucer, spilling a little.

'Jolene,' he said.

She looked at him enquiringly, innocently: 'Mr Eugene?'

He squared the sheaf of paper on his desk and took out a fountain pen. He frowned at the pen as he unscrewed it. An impression of kindness, of absent-mindedness, filtered through her. He was obviously a clever man.

'If you need any help with your studies,' he said, 'please don't hesitate to ask me.'

'Thank you, Mr Eugene.'

Something rarefied the air between them, a feeling other than her amusement. It made breathing difficult; she was reluctant to go. But there was nothing more to keep her.

As she reached the door, he said quietly, 'Jolene Galant.'

She turned, and he asked, 'Your surname is Galant, isn't it?'

'Yes, Sir.'

'I thought so.'

He smoothed the blank sheet of paper in front of him with his thumb. There was an awkward silence. She liked his eyes. They were kind. She caught herself looking directly into them, far too long. He blinked and turned away, shaking his head in something like puzzlement.

Back on her hands and knees in the passage, she is hypnotised by the smell of Cobra wax, by the rhythms of the brush. Her heart beats slowly, its intensity underscoring the single overwhelming question that circles round the circular movement of her hands: what are you doing, woman? What on earth do you think you're doing, what are you doing to yourself messing round with a white man?

Mrs Carelse brought us tea. 'It's not often that we have a guest such as yourself,' she said brightly, more for Jolene Cornick's benefit than mine. Speaking loudly, with the exaggerated animation that comes with treating the old like cretins, she said to Jolene: 'Aren't you lucky today, my dear! You've got a guest!'

'Yerrs...' replied Jolene, without conviction. She sat slumped on the bed, her hands dangled in her lap, her thin cheeks, her dewlap dragging.

'And I've brought you some extra biscuits, yes!'

Jolene looked into whatever vistas the wall offered.

'Will you pour it?' Mrs Carelse asked me. 'I think just now. The tea should draw a little.'

I thanked her and she bustled out.

'It's just because you're here,' said Jolene with a grey smile that fell back quickly to her hangdog looseness. 'She never brings tea, we only get tea from the urn in the sitting room.'

'Shall I be mum?' I asked brightly.

She ignored my suggestion, just continued looking at the wall behind me. I poured the tea anyway and offered her the plate of biscuits. Her hand hovered over a zoo cracker — 'Can't eat that, it's too hard' — and swerved to a finger biscuit.

She dipped it into her tea. I watched her with faint revulsion as she actually sucked the softened part of the biscuit into her mouth. They were called 'boudoir biscuits' I remembered; then the bulge of her tongue ran round the gums, polishing off them that milky pudding.

This is the real conclusion, I thought, subtly repelled, of her love story: a failing body and mind.

I was reminded. 'I've got something for you,' I said. 'Here, in my bag.' I took out the photograph my mother had sent me, the image of Jolene Galant as she was nearly sixty years before.

'What's this?' she asked, holding it at a distance, blinking, peering at it. 'My eyes are very good, you know. That's one thing the good Lord has spared me. Some of the other ladies here, they ask me to thread the needle. And they're younger than me, a lot of them.' She blinked and held the picture even further away. 'Who's this?'

Then suddenly she was grinning toothlessly.

I covertly watched her amused disbelief as she clucked and shook her head. What was it like to be so old? It would happen to me too, I realised. I hunched over and dangled my hands in my lap. I let my jaw hang slack. I imagined my teeth away and ran my tongue around the base of my gums, trying to feel them baby smooth, chewed to flat spalp. And my meagre beauty? Look at her, who had so much more to start off with!

She was staring at me. Had she read my mind? Was I caught out? Betraying fire raged in my fingertips, in my earlobes, turning my cheeks to crimson embers. I took the photograph from her shaking hand.

She stands holding a pot of coffee in the garden on that warm winter Sunday. Sunlight falls on her face, dyeing her skin a pleasant lethargic colour that sinks in ever deeper, spreading through vein and artery to everything she is.

'No,' says Eugene Kruger, lowering Anfra's new camera and looking at her directly. 'It's making too much shadow, see. Stand over there, Jolene.'

She moves. This time the sun falls obliquely from her left. He makes a great deal of peering through the camera. She watches him watching her through the square in the little silver box. It makes her happy: she wants to smile, but doesn't. An inner warmth radiates from her features. And what does Mr Eugene see, looking at her through that thing?

Mr Koen shouted out rudely — so rude, so aggressive,

she jumped: 'What do you think you're doing, Eugene? Aren't you tired of taking snapshots of the maid? I thought you were going to photograph us!'

'Hold your horses, Koen,' said Eugene equably. 'I don't want to give black eyes to the lot of you.'

Koen sat in a group with Mrs Kruger, their old father Mr Barend Sieberhagen who was visiting, and Mr and Mrs Viljoen, who employed Jolene's sister.

'No,' declared Eugene. 'Jolene, would you mind standing over there?'

She moved again. Her arms were beginning to ache. Couldn't he see she was holding a tray?

He was stuck behind that camera. A wave of amusement crashed through her, and she smiled at him. He seemed to go still — washed by pale sunlight, he looked at first very clean, then transparent — as if she could see his memories, his life from inside.

'Did Mr Eugene say something?' she asked. She felt elated. He didn't reply. The moment was gone, vanished into other moments, replaced by simple things: greenery, bare fruit trees, five people sitting lazily in a garden waiting to be photographed, her tired arms. She heard the camera click.

'Yes!' he said. 'That is the spot.'

'Has Mr Eugene finished?' she asked. 'Can I put the coffee down now?'

'Yes, thank you, Jolene,' he said. He pointed to her: 'That is the right place to sit for the picture.'

With humorous groans and exclamations the group lifted their chairs and rearranged themselves.

'Join us, Eugene!' cried Anfra gaily, waving him nearer. 'Let Jolene take the picture!'

'No, Madam!' exclaimed Jolene in horror: 'I can't take the photo, I don't know how to work that thing!'

Eugene smiled and took the photograph himself.

Posterity shows another picture, taken moments before. Her discomfort, the poor photographic quality, the scratches fail to obscure her sleek beauty, her high blank cheekbones, dark eyes, full lips. The structure of her face suggests San or Khoi blood: in her features a delicacy that only just fails to be perfect.

She retires to the back yard with a plate of cake and a tin mug of lukewarm coffee. She sits on the step leading to her room, her back resting against the sun-warmed door, slowly eating her cake, luxuriating in its uncommon sweetness. She closes her eyes and lets warmth invade her body. She stretches out her legs lazily, comfortably. Her mind is filled with an image of Eugene Kruger stooping behind the silver camera. Not all the gentle physical heat she feels comes from the sun.

I watched the spindles turn. We were getting nowhere. Generalisations about how nice my grandparents were, how hard it was to get jobs, stray memories of insignificant particulars, things my grandmother said, even a recipe for steak-and-kidney pie that Anfra often used.

'They don't make it here,' she said. 'They don't make steak-and-kidney pie. I can't eat it.' That pink-gummed smile again: 'Too hard for me.'

Could I be this intrusive? Gatecrash her privacy? I did: 'They say that you had an affair — you were romantically involved — with my grandfather?'

'No, all that stories was very *exaggerated*,' said Mrs Jolene Cornick, showing her first sign of intensity: 'Mr Eugene, he was a very nice man, and it's true, he was very good to me. But it's all nonsense, that stories. You know, Miss Jessica, people *gossip*. They gossip all day long because they got nothing to think about. They gossip, and they make up this *rubbish*. It's just a lot of *nonsense*.'

Here is a different beginning, an eternal present cut out of history. Here is Eugene, restless during the book-keeping lesson. Whenever she looks up, he is staring at her. His eyes slide away, reddened and embarrassed; it alerts her to trouble. The tension has become painful, something you can touch. Then he is behind her — she almost stops breathing — his hands are on her shoulders. She freezes.

'Please, Jolene,' he says, 'Be merciful, I must —'

There is the slow thudding of her heart. She doesn't know what she wants. That paralyses her. Can she accept this? Maybe she admires Mr Eugene, maybe she is drawn to him. But she doesn't want to destroy the simplicity of her life, that one frail protection left. Once it is gone, once that veil is torn —

He makes her stand up, the force of his action bruising her soul.

'Mr Eugene, I can't, I don't, please Mr Eugene —'

So her voice goes on. His hand is inside her clothing, touching her. They keep very still. There is only breathing. She cannot decide what she wants. She makes no decision.

He presses her forwards, gently, insistently, forcing her at last down over the table. She tries to resist but his strength and her anomie are too great to overcome. The arching pressure of her body goes lame, collapses suddenly as all volition, all capacity is crowded out. Things go silver-white, she can't see and maybe — she isn't sure — she passes out briefly. She comes to with his hand, his fingers inside her. She hears the noises her body makes as if that passion isn't her own, and as vision returns she comes to herself moving with his movement.

'Don't do this, Mr Eugene,' she whispers, 'please, please don't do this to me.'

It is far too late for any decisions. He is pressing himself inside her, a slow burning parting of her flesh, but not reluctant.

'I love you,' he whispers, his voice strangling with shame. She has to rock with the painful thrusting. There is no time to it. 'But not here,' he says. He withdraws, lets her up and leads her through the house, bumping her into furniture, through the kitchen and the dark yard to her room. She catches a glimpse of his face in that rush. She knows him as a kind, intelligent man, but now he appears swollen and clumsy, without grace.

In the darkness of her room, on the bed, she is thrown onto all fours and he continues what he has started. It is still painful and difficult to move with him. She reaches behind, grasps and keeps him still — 'Mr Eugene is so tall,' she says — adjusting her own position. He is able to listen to her at last and modifies his movement. It is easier after that, and soon over.

They lie together under her blankets. She has no sheets. The bed is crowded with the sharp scents of sweat, of sex. His breath, his hair, even his skin, smell of coffee and cheroot. Eugene Kruger doesn't say a word to her. He drapes his arm loosely round her body. She keeps very still and waits for history to move forward.

'Jolene, I think Mrs Kruger will be back from her Bible class quite soon,' he says. He gets up, pulls up his trousers hastily, fumbles with his buckle, leaves. Jolene rolls over onto her back and lies with her eyes open, staring up into darkness.

2

I sat talking to him as he sliced the pale leeks. The blade projecting from those plump fingers moved with surprising precision and speed.

'I don't know, Teboso, I don't know.'

He scooped a tablespoon of chopped garlic into hot olive oil. It started spitting immediately, the aroma filling his little kitchen. He threw in the sliced leeks and dusted off his hands with enormous satisfaction.

'When you cook, you must get involved,' he declared. 'Sometimes I feel like singing to the food.' He took a wooden spoon and began humming as he stirred, quite ostentatiously, in case I missed the point.

'There is such a discrepancy between what Jolene Cornick says and what Koen Sieberhagen says. I don't know... it's frustrating, Teboso. It's damn frustrating.'

He brandished the spoon. 'Do you know that leeks and onions, and garlic and so on — spring onions — they're all lilies? Consider the lilies of the field! These are most salacious foods!'

Salutary foods? Healthy foods? Libidinous foods?

I said: 'Butter wouldn't melt in her mouth! She blinks her vapid eyes and mumbles a lot of inanities. I can't bear it anymore.'

'Why do you think,' he retorted, 'she should do anything else?'

'Well — because, because —'

'Why should she talk to you in the first place? Why on earth should she expose her life, her secrets, her intimate past? No, I am serious. You must examine your expectations, Jessica. You must explore your rationale for this investigation, this oral history of yours! Is it an investigation of the settler colony, or an extension of it?'

'I can't think of any reason why she should confide in me,' I replied. 'I doubt she can remember her secrets anyway.'

When he had added the diced, peeled and seeded tomatoes, and the red wine and the tomato paste, and the basil fresh out of his window box, and the sublimated wine had risen heavenly into the atmosphere of the kitchen, I said, 'That leaves me nowhere. I've still got to do this. I've still got to pry it out of her somehow. I've got to pry something out of her. I don't care about her extinct love-life anymore. I couldn't even get any substantial information about her wages. Or about her hours of work. Her relationship with her employers — I mean her economic relationship. Nothing! Zilch! I did get a recipe for steak-and-kidney pie...'

He tasted the sauce and added sugar. He tasted again and added more wine. He dipped his fingers into a container of pitted olives and dropped them into the saucepan. Oil dripped off his hand, now slick, aubergine. He flicked it over the food. 'Nothing like olives,' he said, sticking his fingertips into his mouth together and sucking off kalamata liquor.

'Pass me that towel, will you,' he requested. I did. He stopped trying to clean his hand eventually and said, 'Make it up, you silly woman. Make it up!'

'I can't do that —'

'No, I don't mean cheat — I mean construct it, infer it, read between the lines, write an imaginative history. Use your imagination as the instrument of knowledge it might one day be!'

'Oh, Teboso,' I sighed. 'So easy to say things like that. My instrument of knowledge is utterly tired out.'

She is washing up in the scullery while he lounges about the kitchen, watching her work, his regard weighing her down; the burden of desire, his raw need, creeps up on her, over her, becomes oppressive. She throws a single resentful glance in his direction and continues washing plates, ignoring him pointedly.

His odour announces his proximity: dark tobacco mixed with the summer smell of a man, strong but not unpleasant. He leans down and kisses her neck. She shies away: 'No!' she whispers urgently. 'No, Mr Eugene! Madam is in the house right now.'

'She's going out tonight, Jolene.'

Her mouth compresses angrily as she continues her work.

'I need you, Jolene. I want you tonight.'

She shakes her head sullenly. 'Mr Eugene can't come. It's my time of the month.'

It isn't true. But she doesn't know how else to oppose him. She feels flimsy, paper-thin. He doesn't believe her, she knows that. The timing is wrong.

She still hears the stones that thundered down on her

roof, the crude voices assaulting darkness, destroying safety, she still suffers the fear of that night, the terror of broken anonymity. But Eugene doesn't care. Can't he see what might happen to her? And doesn't he care that Anfra is still in the house? She feels stifled by his carelessness, by his growing indifference to everything except the thing he desires.

'I see,' he says finally, churlish in the face of her silence. When she looks round again he has gone.

She finishes up and goes to her room, taking her tin plate of stew. She eats in candle-lit silence, anxious and lonely, without appetite.

There is a knock on the door. Eugene, of course. She opens up a few inches. Light spilling from behind her paints a warm swathe down half his face, leaving the rest shadowed.

'I need you, Jolene. I want to come in.'

She shakes her head. He leans forward and kisses her full on the mouth. She tolerates it, draws back.

He pushes the door wide open, easily brushing her out of the way.

She backs away, staring at him, startled, cautious.

'Don't look at me like that,' he says, taking her shoulders in his large hands. 'I can't bear it. You are too beautiful.'

When she speaks at last, it isn't in the voice of a servant: 'This must stop, Mr Eugene.'

He bends down and kisses her neck, her face, wrapping his arms about her, almost bruising her back and ribs. She pushes him away vigorously, struggling to get out of his embrace. He is too powerful for her. She goes limp and sags against him. He takes it for capitulation and partly releases her, brushing his hand across her face gently.

'I love you, Jolene,' he whispers. 'I really love you. I don't know how or why, but no one — not even my wife —'

As they go down he knocks the candle over. The back of her hand comes down on it. A brief searing of flesh, the flame is extinguished. She is angry now, violently angry and awake and alive for the first time in the history of their loving. The pain of her hand and the pain of being used are indistinguishable. She lies with her eyes open and cold as he moves upon her.

'No more, Mr Eugene,' she says hoarsely. 'I can't do this anymore.'

He gets up slowly, clumsily, recovering his breath, reaching for his trousers. She wipes herself down angrily with her bedclothes.

'Alright,' he says, releasing a long, tense sigh. 'Alright, Jolene, alright.'

He buckles his fly and fastens his belt, moving wearily.

'Thank you,' he says, his voice grave and gentle. 'Thank you for everything, Jolene.'

She remains where she is, kneeling on the mattress, still naked, unable to speak. She knows then that she will have to leave. He knows it too.

Before she can react, another voice speaks for her, shattering their secrecy — it is Anfra, calling her name gently, just outside the wide open door, peering in uncertainly. This is one thing she will never forget. Anfra's face, melting down at the point of revelation: the cruelty of her shock, the way agony distorts her features.

I returned the next Saturday, bringing Mrs Cornick a large box of chocolates. I made sure they were soft-centred. She placed the box on her lap with absent dignity and waited in a passive silence.

As I fiddled with the recorder, making sure it was working, she said, 'Your grandmother, is she still alive?'

Mrs Cornick's memory was obviously failing — I had given her that information. 'Yes,' I replied. 'But unfortunately senile. Her world is very small now.'

She nodded, still impassive.

'Your grandfather, is he alive now?'

'No, Mrs Cornick. He died many years ago.'

She retreated into her silence. Then a small dispirited laugh crept up out of her, and she said, 'I don't remember him. I can't remember what he looks like.'

I stared at her uncomfortably.

'Well now,' she said, and I put the recorder back on the table and straightened up and braced myself to continue wrestling with her surprisingly muscular reticence, her patient, unmovable muteness.

I thought I would try a different tack, naively hoping the truth would come out if I used indirect questioning methods.

'Mrs Cornick, why did you leave the employ of my grandparents?'

She sat clutching the box of chocolates, staring a little past me.

'Mrs Cornick?'

She prepared her lips to speak in the manner I had become used to. Eventually it came out: 'You know, Miss Jessica, I'm happy with my lot now and I thank God every day because I've got a warm place to sleep, and I've got good food to eat, and I've got very nice friends. I'm lucky. I'm very happy here.'

Was her mind wandering?

'Mrs Cornick?' I repeated. 'I asked why you left the employ of my grandparents.'

Her gaze swung away from the wall. She looked at me in a watery kind of way, blinking.

'Sorry, Mrs Cornick. I was just wanting to know — did you leave the employ of my grandparents for any — for any particular reason?'

'Your grandparents, they was very good to me.'

'Please call me Jessica,' I said, trying to hide my exasperation. 'I would feel much more comfortable.'

She nodded. She relapsed into silence. Then there was an almost visible mental effort, she gathered herself and returned her attention to me. 'I didn't want to leave them,' she said. She shrugged. 'But Mr Koen Sieberhagen, he offered me quite good wages at the time. He wanted me to look after his farmhouse. There was nobody living there.'

'So it was just a question of wages? You had no more pressing or compelling reason to leave?'

'Yerrs,' she said, her voice whistling, trailing off into that silence in which she seemed to hide herself. Weakly, distantly, she added, 'There was nothing special about it. I just went to work for Mr Koen. But I didn't stay there long.'

Koen's car bucks and slews along the muddy driveway. Bullrushes, wild grasses bowed with heavy ears of seed dripping resin, thickets of oleander, argumentative clumps of wattle line the route. Jolene sits in the back seat as is proper for a maid, holding tightly to the armrest.

The back of Koen's head annoys her. It sprouts from his shoulders rigidly, with an arrogance that sets her teeth on edge. It is a crude arrogance.

The rear end of the car slid wildly to the right, they lurched to a halt. Koen lost his temper and gunned the engine. The wheels spun helplessly. He swore and got out the car. He kneeled below Jolene's door, examining the back wheel.

She sat inside and waited. The heat mounted.

Her door burst open; she looked up at his angry, red, sweating face.

'Come,' he said, and walked off.

'Mr Koen?' she had to yell after him. He was already twenty paces down the road. 'What about my things?'

'We're not far, bring it,' he shouted, without looking back.

She picked up her sorry remnants of a suitcase and followed him.

They were already in the farm driveway. But after only a hundred yards, she was wet through — it was a distressingly humid day — her shoes were coated with slimy orange mud. She struggled on, breathing heavily, her case banging against her legs.

Koen was soon out of sight around the bend. She stopped to catch her breath. Fleshy plants with giant heart-shaped leaves lined the road here, radiating their intense emerald. It was hard to breathe in the violence of that colour.

A great racketing cry fell from the sky, released by a flight of ibis. It temporarily interrupted the constant manic clatter of guinea fowl, then they picked up the beat again. Where am I? she thought. What is this place? The cloying smell of stagnant water rose from the ditch pacing the driveway, midges swarmed everywhere. She wiped her sleeve across her forehead and continued, picking a careful path through the mud.

The driveway released her, and there lay the barnlike hulk of the farmhouse, the shutters sagging, the door open. A black tin roof, an attic with broken windows extending over the whole frame; the grounds neglected, rich with spiderwebs and insect life, rife with the scents of broken and blossoming vegetation. Beside the house were two cement dams, choked to bubbling with algae and bluegum pollen.

There was no sign of Koen. She walked up the steps into the merciful shade of the porch. A dull brass plate beside the door bore the legend: Daljosafat. She knocked timidly. There was no reply, so she set her case down, took her shoes off and entered.

She couldn't see at first. The house was built with the heat in mind. The walls were eighteen inches thick, the ceilings at least twelve feet high, and lined with reeds. The smell of dust was heavy.

Koen appeared out of the darkness of the interior. 'There you are,' he said. 'Come.' He beckoned. 'Look, Jolene, you can dust the place for me. Just keep it clean, more or less, but don't worry too much. Open the windows every day, close them at night.'

Inside the house, where it was darker and cooler, he looked different — less angry, less likely to burst out of his skin.

'I just don't want anyone breaking in. That's why I'm leaving you here. I don't want the locals to think this place is deserted. Now listen, I haven't found any labourers for this farm yet. There's just an old couple — his name is Gideon, I don't know his woman's name — in the worker's cottages. You know where that is?'

She shook her head.

He ignored her denial. 'If you need anything, you can call on them, see? I know him, he's a good man, he's worked for me before. Let me show you round quickly before I leave. I've got to get that damn car out of the ditch.'

He took her round the deserted farmhouse. There was a cavernous inner room. Its only access to light was through the entrance hall, the doors of the bedrooms which front-ed it, and the doors on the oppposing wall that led to the kitchen and to an adjoining enclosed porch.

Each of the front rooms had a single window, tall and narrow, the sill about knee height. He opened the sash win-dows and the shutters for her. 'I'm going to replant the whole lot,' he said, gesturing at the vines outside. 'There's more weeds than vine-stock there.' He looked at her with-out interest. 'Raisins,' he said, 'You eat raisins?'

'I like raisins, Mr Koen.'

He nodded and walked out of the room. She followed. He took her back through the inner chamber to the kitchen. The large table in the centre was the only piece of furniture in the house. The kitchen was bare, lacking even a stove. There were no fewer than three doors leading out into a bewildering series of outhouses, sculleries, small irregular service rooms with windows of various shapes and sizes. Squatting in the centre of that maze, an enormous baker's oven. Koen grinned: 'You can sleep there if you like.'

He promised to come back with provisions once he had got the car out of the ditch, and left her alone with the keys in that giant farmhouse.

She kept inside most of the time. It was too hot outside.

Light came in through the cracks in the shutters, rays projected through dusty air. As the day went on, these rays of light changed angle slowly, with infinite patience. That was her only measure of time, other than the insane mechanical cackle of guinea fowl, and the sweeter trolling of doves.

Koen returned much later with a brown paper bag containing milk and bread, cheese, tinned meat. He also brought matches and candles, blankets, and eating utensils. 'I'll get you a Primus later,' he said. 'Maybe tomorrow. Then you can make coffee and tea.'

He left, taking his disturbing presence with him.

That was the only interruption. He had shown her the well behind the kitchen with its brass pump handle. It delivered sweet, ice-cold water. From time to time she would go there and drink, not because she was thirsty, but because it was something to do.

At sunset she sat on the steps of the house with a plate of food, looking over the vineyard. Gnarled black vines rose out of the chalky soil, sprouting fringes of spring leaves. Her reverie was interrupted when a pair of Egyptian geese slid over the roof with a hissing archery of wings and arrowed away over the vineyards. There were large, noisy birds here: guinea fowl, geese, *hadeda* ibis, crows rowing across the evening sky with slow liquid strokes. As darkness gathered the bats swung out, looping erratically in front of the house, trying to terrify her. Full darkness brought giant hawkmoths, their dense bodies blurring in swift short lines of flight. One singed itself on her candle with a sputtering of wax, and crashed to the floor, its wings vibrating horribly. She jumped up with a thrill of revulsion and went inside.

She wandered from room to room, not frightened, but feeling hollow. The centre room made her particularly uneasy. She settled her blankets eventually in one of the front rooms. Then she placed her candle on the floor and sat with her back to the wall. She fell asleep in that position and later slid over onto her side. She dreamt of Eugene and

Anfra, feverish, angry, accusing dreams. She woke in pain, her bones sore from the hard floor, her head aching. She looked around wildly, trying to work out where she was; then frowned at the guttering candle, the leaping shadows it caused.

She crawled on hands and knees towards the candle, to blow it out. There, caught and lost by the leaping penumbra was something concentrated, something red — she lifted the candle to see what it was. A baboon spider drifted along the dust, a red-furred hunter big enough to overspread her palm. It was the last straw. Shaking, she scrambled up, trying to gather her blankets in one hand, still holding the candle in the other. She skirted the spider and ran out the room, trailing her blankets in the dust, the candle guttering frantically. It went out in the centre chamber, leaving her in darkness with a pounding heart, a fat smell of tallowsmoke, the great thick-walled hulk closing around her like a whale that had swallowed her whole.

Three days passed with infinite slowness. She had never known leisure. It was hard to do next to nothing: it felt unnatural.

Koen arrived on the second with more provisions. He had even dredged up a coir mattress and a pillow. The mattress smelt foul, so she didn't use it.

Exploring the property after he left, she discovered a large earthwork dam not far from the house. Surmounting the wall, she surprised wild duck, mallard flashing green and salmon into the air. Her heart soared with them as she absorbed the view: green water unevenly surrounded by clumps of bullrushes, shaded on the eastern side by a screen of black wattle. Here and there, an islet broke the surface. Beyond the dam, a patchwork quilt of orchards and vineyards spread to the mountains separating the valley from the rest of Africa. She longed to cool down in the dam, but couldn't swim. Late that evening she came, stripped and gingerly waded in. But the clay was slippery and sloped too steeply down to the unknown depth. It was too great a risk.

She sleeps on the kitchen table, the only place in the house elevated above floor level, dreaming she is a traveller in a desert land, searching for water. She probes the roots of desert shrubs and succulents with a sharpened stick. Only sand, roots and tubers, more sand. Then — as footsteps intrude on her sleep — she finds what she is looking for: a cache of stoppered ostrich eggs, each filled with water. She raises one and drinks deep the warm liquor.

Koen stood in the room, carrying a hurricane lamp in one hand, a bottle of brandy in the other. He stood where he was, weaving. He gestured with the bottle.

'Hello, Jolene,' he said. He took a few steps forward and put the lantern down on the floor. He raised the bottle to his lips, tilted his head back and drank; drew a hissing breath in through his teeth, let it out slowly.

'You're a damn good-looking woman,' he said. 'Eugene ever tell you that?'

She had raised herself on her elbow. Now she swung her legs off the table, pulling the blanket around her shoulders, feeling very exposed.

'Why Eugene?' he asked. 'He's a dry stick. How come a good-looking lady like you got stuck with a stick like Eugene?'

He offered her the bottle. 'Drink?'

She shook her head.

'Mind if I sit down?' he asked. Then, slurring: 'Thank you so much.' He retreated, slid down against the wall. Jolene sat on the table, unsure what to make of him.

'Do you believe in evolution?' he asked. 'You know, the theory of evolution?'

She shook her head again, eyes wide.

'Let me explain it to you. Evolution, that means going forward. Do you believe in it? I do, I believe in — in going forward. It means you have progress in life.'

He took a long, effortless drink of neat brandy — she couldn't believe her eyes — and said, 'It's a question of hierarchy. You know what that means? It means order. Hierarchy means order, running up and down like a ladder. Man is superior to woman. White is superior to coloured, and so on. What do you think of that, Jolene?'

She said nothing. Slowly, carefully, she began to ease herself off the table.

'That's hierarchy,' explained Koen. 'If you don't have hierarchy, you have anarchy. Anarchy means chaos. Chaos, that means no order. You understand?'

He sighed sadly. 'To be honest, Jolene, I'm not sure where I stand on this ladder. I can't tell. I don't have much order left.'

His head settled back against the wall, and he closed his eyes. He stayed like that, breathing heavily. A single snore escaped. She was on her feet now, unsure what to do. He jerked awake again: 'Long day, Jolene. Good looking.'

He placed his hand round the doorpost behind him and tried to get up. He lurched back. 'God,' he said, 'getting old — haven't had that much —'

He pushed himself forward onto his knees, and from there he rose more easily, taking the brandy with him.

He took a few steps into the room and stopped. 'Hierarchy is nature,' he said. 'You have predators and you have the prey — that means the animals the predators hunt and kill. You have leopards and you have baboons. You can't tell me a baboon is superior to a leopard. God made things that way.'

He was standing straight, arms dangling at his sides. The bottle slipped out of his hands and broke, the smell of brandy rapidly tainting the air. 'Damn,' he said. 'Clumsy.'

He came forward, right up to her. 'What do you think, Jolene? Of all this evolution?' He reached down and raised her chin.

'Look at me,' he said. 'You know in your heart this is true. That's why you're looking away from me right now.

You know where you stand in this order. You know in your heart, you know in your own heart —'

He let her go and straightened up, suddenly moral. He said: 'You know in your own heart that what you and Eugene Kruger did together was wrong. You cheated my sister and you mated with a white man. That's why you fear to look at me.'

He pointed at his own chest and thumped his forefinger against it emphatically as he spoke: 'But you don't fear to look at me because *I* say it's wrong. You fear to look at me because behind me, standing behind me you see the image of your God.'

There was fear in her eyes: she thought he had gone mad.

'I don't mean I look like God, or God looks like me, don't get me wrong. I don't mean it like that. But what I mean is —'

He frowned and tried again: 'What I mean is that — that God is a white man. Oh, yes. He's a white man and he's going to judge you for what you do.'

He shook his head in denial. 'Not me, Jolene, not me. I'm not going to judge you, see, I don't judge anyone. I like you. I like you very much. I was just telling you how — how it is.'

His face burned vividly into her senses: a poisoned white, his eyes dead, his forehead beaded with sweat.

He began taking off his belt. 'Come now, Jolene.'

She watched him, paralysed.

'I'm not much worse than Eugene, am I? Not very different to Eugene.' He laughed as a joke occurred to him: 'Just another stiff white cock, that's all, what's the difference?'

He raised one leg to take off his boot. He struggled with it, hopping about, then sat down carefully. He unlaced it and succeeded in removing the boot. The other followed. Now he was barefoot: no socks, his feet white and wrinkled.

She circled around him cautiously; he stopped her in her tracks with a single pointed finger. It was a sign that assumed everything, took for granted his right, his power, his will to command and to possess her.

She kept still.

He stood up suddenly despite his extreme drunkenness and unbuttoned his trousers. They dropped to his ankles. No underwear either. He stepped out of his pants and approached her. He laughed again and said, 'Close your eyes and think of Eugene.'

A gale of anger overwhelmed her, rising out of everything she had experienced. It was his turn to stop, surprised by her sudden crouching intensity, her eyes flattening in rage.

'Ag, come now, my darling,' he crooned, 'don't be like that. Come now to Koen, come here to old Koen.'

He clutched at her blanket, trying ineffectually to pull it off, pursing his lips in kissing motions. She nearly vomited with revulsion.

'Fuck you!' she heard herself shout, right into his face. She placed her hands on his chest and pushed him away violently: 'Fuck you, Mr Eugene!'

She will not forget his expression as he stares at her and says, 'I am not Eugene —'

And this is another thing Jolene will never forget: Koen tottering backwards, his foot coming down on broken glass. 'Jesus,' he says, 'sweet Jesus,' lifting his foot and staring at her reproachfully, as if it were her fault. And it is not only the injury, she sees, that upsets him: his feelings are hurt.

It is to be her last image of Koen, left behind as she walks round him hastily — not in fear — out through the brÔoding room in the middle of the house, out through the open front door, into the luminous night.

'We girls are letting our hair down,' said Natasha Goldman. 'We shall have a hen party like this every second Tuesday to let our hair down more regularly. Or is it a chicken party? — I forget which.'

She sat with her feet on Teboso's balcony, overlooking the red tiled roofs of Observatory, a bottle of Amstel in her hand. Teboso was at his desk marking essays, separated from us only by the window.

Natasha wore sunglasses, of course. The fact that the sun was down didn't matter. The lenses were indigo blue, the frames a kind of psychedelic tortoise shell. '*Mes nouvelles lunettes*,' she had pronounced as I stood in the doorway blinking and warding my eyes, '*un peu flamboyantes*.' Then added: 'My rainbow nation shades.'

'I don't think I've been called a hen before,' I said now. 'Cow, perhaps, but not hen.'

'By the way,' she asked, waving her bottle vaguely in my direction, 'what happened to that silly history project you were doing?'

'Oh, that. I finished it eventually. With great difficulty. Handed it in.'

'And what was so *greatly* difficult?'

'The survivors of that history, my so-called sources. I couldn't get a thing out of them. Evasive, half-senile, obtuse to the bitter end. They contradicted each other wherever possible. In the end I had to hand in such a skimpy excuse of a project that I'll get a third if I'm lucky.'

Natasha pondered, looking deeply into the mouth of her bottle. 'You should have disguised yourself as a black student,' she said. 'Maybe you could have called yourself Ms Ngqayimbana. You should have scribbled something illegible in ballpoint, and very short, and handed it in saying that there was a power failure in Guguletu the night before. Then you would be sure to get at least, at least — oh, I would say seventy-five per cent!'

For some reason, this struck a nerve. We shrieked with laughter; then I turned scarlet as I realised that Teboso might have overheard this racist humour. I swivelled round to look at him. There he was, ballpoint in hand, pensive expression on his face, looking straight at me. Had he heard? I couldn't tell. I turned round again, uneasily. We continued joking and drinking. The sky continued to darken. Teboso Nquayimbana continued to work behind the plate glass sheet, his stout figure obscured by the reflections on its surface.

Here is Jolene Galant walking down the dirt road from the farm Daljosafat, in the night, under a glaring moon, free of history. She walks swiftly. Beside the road grow giant exploding banks of white moonflowers, morning glory dark under moonlight, row upon row of oleander, thorny streamers of wild dog rose. The night is loud with cricket song and cicada, the air is cool on her skin. It is many miles to her home in Pniel from here, but Jolene will walk on till she gets there, if it takes ninety or even a hundred full years.